ROUSSEAU'S GARDEN

by

Ann Charney

THE PERMANENT PRESS
SAG HARBOR, NY 11963

Library of Congress Cataloging-in-Publication Data

Charney, Ann
    Rousseau's Garden: a novel / by Ann Charney
      p. cm.
    ISBN 1-57962-033-7 (alk. paper)
    1. Women photographers--Fiction. 2. Rousseau, Jean-
Jacques--Fiction. 3. Ermenonville (France)--Fiction.
4. Canadians--France--Fiction. 5. Mothers--Death--Fiction.
6. Paris (France)--Fiction. 7. Married women--Fiction.
I. Title.

PR9199.3.C4745 R68 2001
813'.54--dc21   00-064273
                                CIP

THE PERMANENT PRESS
4170 Noyac Road
Sag Harbor, NY 11963

"On dirait que mon coeur et esprit
n'appartiennent pas au même individu."

Jean Jacques Rousseau

ONE

A crisp March morning in the Buttes-Chaumont park. Claire Symons, waiting to meet her husband Adrian, had more than a tourist's passing interest in the place. These acres of greenery in the heart of Paris were linked to a childhood memory suffused with a sense of irrepressible happiness.

Claire needed all the sunny memories she could find. Lately, sudden spasms of apprehension ambushed her in the most ordinary of circumstances. In her worst moments, Claire, who was a successful photographer, had been forced to abandon work in mid-session — unable to account for her actions to those around her. It could have been funny if it hadn't been so scary. A grown woman bolting like a nervous cat, spooked by something in the darkness no human eye could see.

And so she had come here looking for a lake where children sailed toy boats. Her mind turned to this innocent comforting scene whenever she felt troubled. The smooth water and the gently gliding boats never failed to soothe her.

Claire had been no more than five or six the first time her mother, Dolly, brought her to Paris. She wasn't certain if her memory belonged to that first visit or to later ones. Dolly, who taught art at a junior college in Montréal and was a well-regarded sculptor, came to Paris regularly to visit her close friend Marta and to look at art. Claire wasn't even sure the memory came from an outing to the Buttes-Chaumont, but she suspected it did. She remembered a rugged background of craggy promontories and densely wooded paths, making it unlikely the scene had taken place in the manicured gardens of the Tuileries or the Luxembourg.

Even as a child Claire had been blessed with an acute visual memory. Her ability to retain visual clues kept her from losing her way in foreign cities, a useful quality for someone whose work involved frequent travel. Her sure sense of direction impressed Adrian when they first met. He was not used to women whose ability to orient themselves surpassed his, he had told her admiringly.

Strolling along the rustic walks of the Buttes-Chaumont, Claire became more certain she was in the right place. She might have missed the lake, however, had she not followed a steep trail to a point of high elevation, giving her a clear view of her surroundings. It was then that she saw water, shimmering as in her memory, and the children playing nearby. She was too far to see the boats but she knew they were there.

She ran towards the lake along a steep curving path, keeping her eye on it as it vanished and reappeared among the trees like a longed-for mirage, until she arrived at its edge. Gazing at the expanse of water, smaller and more contained than she remembered, she felt the presence of the past enclose her like a soft familiar blanket.

Once again she heard her mother's comforting voice and felt her mother's hand on hers as she struggled to navigate the rented sailboat with the long pole she had been given. After a few awkward attempts Claire grew discouraged. It didn't help seeing the French children all around her handling theirs with such ease. But Dolly stayed close, the soft sleeve of her sweater brushing Claire's cheek, guiding Claire's movements until she got the hang of it. She could still hear her mother's shouts of pleasure and feel her arms, strong from the hours she spent building her wooden forms, lifting her off the ground and swinging her around in a triumphant dance. Then, side by side, they proudly watched their boat sail forward to join the miniature French flotilla.

Walking along the rim of the lake, she wondered what it was about that day long ago in the Buttes-Chaumont that made it so vivid. Why had it survived when so many other happy moments with her mother had faded? The mind was like an earthquake zone, she thought, each emotional tremor burying more of the terrain. No wonder she held on to that memory as if it were a precious relic.

When she had first heard Adrian's stories about growing up in the midst of the large, closely-knit Arensberg clan, she had been astonished by their richness and variety. Her own family recollections were sparse, painful, and difficult to tell. Adrian Arensberg came to her embellished by the vivid colors of his past; all she could offer was her meager self. He had laughed at her notions and warned her that his family would seem less romantic up close. Adrian had been right, Claire soon discovered. The members of Adrian's family seemed to prefer their own company to all others, filling their social calendar with endless rounds of celebration, as if the family practiced a private religion requiring strict observance. He advised her not to convert.

She smiled, thinking of Adrian, and checked her watch. He was late. They had been married three years, long enough for Claire not to be surprised. In deference to Claire, Adrian's watch was now set fifteen minutes ahead, but his natural tardiness seemed to outwit this ploy as well. Her own "compulsive promptness" — Adrian's words — did not help matters.

Everything about Adrian had pleased her when they first met: his short curly hair, his agile, compact body, his even temper, his reassuring competence. She even liked his voice, so low it forced her to lean towards him to hear his words. So it had come as a shock to discover that the man she admired was incapable of arriving on time.

Adrian's deficiency, she learned, did not indicate indifference or rudeness. Life simply conspired to throw up detours along his path, undermining his best intentions. She had a chance to see how the sabotage worked soon after they met. She'd spent the night at Adrian's flat and he had offered to drive her back to her place in the morning so that she could change her clothes before heading out on an assignment. A magazine had commissioned her to photograph a racing car driver who had just won an international meet. She and Adrian were still at the tentative stage where it would have seemed presumptuous to bring along a change of clothes.

She wasn't thinking of her assignment when she awoke. Instead, sipping tea from one of Adrian's translucent blue cups, she brooded about her unusual state of well-being. She was used to difficult, demanding lovers whose presence left her with an irresistible urge to be alone. This new feeling of contentment made her uneasy. Her response to Adrian was too good, too quick, too sane. She felt like someone in a heavy winter overcoat surprised by sudden warm weather. Adrian, sitting across from her, appeared untroubled as he went through the morning mail. He looked neat and alert although less than an hour earlier he had been sleeping so soundly beside her, she had been reluctant to wake him.

"What's this?" he asked, holding up a letter he had just pulled from the pile of mail in front of him. "Wrong name, wrong address. Can't imagine how it got here and now it's too late to catch the mailman. You don't mind if we drop it off on our way?" He slipped the letter into the inside pocket of his wool jacket before Claire could answer. She would have simply dropped the letter in a mailbox and forgotten it, but she said nothing. A man who went out of his way to deliver a letter to a stranger was worth a few minutes' wait.

Of course, it turned out to be more than a few minutes. Adrian was not very good at estimating time. And there was the morning traffic that made their progress even slower. None of it mattered, however. Claire would have been happy to remain with Adrian for the rest of the day trapped in stalled traffic and serenaded by the horns of impatient drivers. She needed the time to sort out her feelings, to assimilate this new proof of his decency. Eventually, she came to see Adrian as a good man at war with punctuality.

In the three years since, her belief in his decency had not wavered and his struggle with time had not improved. She had simply learned to allow for his lateness. She found a pleasant spot to wait and reached for the book she had brought along, a selection of letters attributed to Jean Jacques Rousseau, the great eighteenth-century French philosopher. It had been given to her by Adrian's friend, Marcel de Berry. The book had been a parting gift at the end of his visit with them in Montréal, a peace offering to make up for behavior even Marcel recognized as excessive.

Marcel's petulance surfaced when he learned that the guestroom he had previously occupied had been converted into a studio and darkroom for Claire. Reluctantly installed in a hotel, Marcel did not hesitate to disturb Claire with repeated nuisance requests: Could she bring laundry detergent when she and Adrian came to take him to dinner that evening? It seemed silly to buy an entire box, he explained, when he only had a couple of shirts and some socks and underwear to wash. Could Claire bring a few plastic hangers? he inquired a few minutes later. The wooden ones in the hotel room would stain his shirts. On other days, he needed an umbrella, a heating pad for his back, something for his headache. Yet, despite his frequent demands, he persisted in ignoring her when they all were together, addressing his remarks only to Adrian.

Adrian Arensberg and Marcel de Berry were both art historians and they had been exchanging ideas for years, ever since their meeting at a conference in Geneva where they had discovered a shared passion for gardens as great works of art. Listening to them, Claire felt as she had the first time Adrian brought her to a gathering of his family. His three sisters, their husbands and children, his aunts, uncles, cousins, all spoke a kind of shorthand dialect she found nearly incomprehensible. Claire, an only child with no close relatives living nearby, had been dazed by their noisy exuberance. She had had some success since then in penetrating the family circle — two of his sisters told her how much happier Adrian seemed since their marriage; the third sister, who still lunched regularly with Adrian's ex-wife, the illustrious Pamela Porter, remained a Pamela loyalist. With Marcel, however, relations had not improved.

Nevertheless, on the last day of his visit, after calling Claire to find out if he could borrow a small traveling case for his new purchases, he surprised her with a gift. The shabby-looking volume, he assured her, was a rare find. The letters were addressed to a woman whose identity was unknown, and there was some doubt about their authenticity.

"These academic quarrels are of no consequence, however, to a reader who reads for the sheer pleasure of the text. You're interested in gardening, I believe? You will find Rousseau — I choose to believe he is the author — a wonderful guide. He was a self-taught botanist, you know, who earned his living as a herbalist."

Had the book been a lucky guess, or had Adrian prompted Marcel?

Adrian knew the strange role the philosopher had played in Claire's early life. "He was my mother's guru, her spiritual adviser," she had flippantly explained when Adrian had inquired about the portrait of Rousseau in her bedroom. Claire had inherited the painting from Dolly — a copy of the famous portrait painted by Allan Ramsay during Rousseau's stay in Scotland — and it accompanied her wherever she moved.

This exchange took place the first time Adrian stayed over in Claire's flat. He had pressed her for an explanation, intrigued by her remark, but she had put him off. Talk about her mother was bound to dissipate the tantalizing sensations Adrian's presence aroused in her. She could not let that happen. Even then, when they barely knew each other, when the sound of his voice on her answering machine still surprised her, she sensed that this quietly intense man, with his intelligent, level gaze, was going to matter a great deal to her. Dolly's story could wait.

In time, Adrian learned how Claire had been raised on Rousseau lore, interpreted by Dolly. Dolly had always insisted, Claire explained, that Rousseau's exaltation of nature provided her with the esthetic impulse to redefine her work as a sculptor. Claire could almost recite Dolly's explanations by heart: she had grown dissatisfied with her early representational figures. Rousseau's work had inspired her treks into the countryside where she sketched natural forms, translating them later in her studio into abstract geometric solids. Claire showed Adrian a statement Dolly had prepared for an exhibition in which she wrote, "With Rousseau as my guide I perceived the energy and movement inherent in each form of nature." When Adrian pressed her for more information, Claire found herself unable to answer. Growing up, she had blocked her ears when her mother spoke of Rousseau. She minded her mother's absences too much to care for her reasons.

Well, she was making amends by reading the book Marcel had given her. Slowly, she was coming to appreciate his gift. Rousseau's voice, emanating from the book's pages like the persistent aroma of a long ago pressed flower, took her by surprise. The querulous tone, filled with self-justification and surprising intimacy, succeeded in holding her attention in a way that Dolly's interpretations never had. Somehow, in his own words, Rousseau sounded far more appealing. Or perhaps she had her own reasons now for being more receptive to the philosopher's voice.

A few pages into the text, however, she grew tired of sitting and decided to walk. Adrian, she remembered, was giving a talk to Marcel's students at the École des Beaux-Arts and would, no doubt, be even later than usual. His lectures on art history were inevitably followed by a rush of

11

admirers, wanting to keep him as long as possible. She had ample time to explore her surroundings.

She was surprised to find a few children and an occasional adult inside grassy enclosures circled by a wire fence bearing the sign *"Pelouse Autorisée."* The peaceful scene reminded her of grazing sheep. She spotted a lone workman nearby, carefully spreading topsoil among tender young shoots, and asked him for an explanation.

"Our mayor has decided to open certain lawns to the public," he said, straightening up. "It's the end of the parks as we know them. Once they start bringing their dogs here, the lawns will turn into fields of garbage, like the city streets."

Claire had seen no sign of such abuse this morning, but the gardener's pessimism alarmed her. The park was still very much as it appeared in the nineteenth-century views sold at the entrance gate. She did not want the Buttes-Chaumont, scene of her childhood idyll, to change.

The well-cared-for landscape soon reassured her. She noted the benches, intact and unvandalized. Orderly strollers spoke to one another in tones that barely disturbed the quiet of the day, permitting Claire to hear the songs of birds hovering somewhere in the thick, newly green treetops. The serenity of the scene was untroubled by booming tape decks, transistor radios or Frisbees flying through the air. Nor was there any sign of menacing figures lurking along the well-kept paths. The French were too proud of their treasured public gardens to permit their ruin, she decided. Even the dogs she passed moved as sedately as their owners. Remembering the gardener's warning, Claire wondered if any of these well-trained animals still retained a flicker of some dormant instinct that could cause them to break rank and tear across the forbidden lawn in a wild spree of abandon. For a moment she wished she could witness such a scene, if only to see the reaction of those around her.

She walked on, thinking how nice it was to have time to contemplate the behavior of dogs and men. She was enjoying this unusual period of idleness thanks to Adrian's new project. He was writing a book on French gardens and his work made it necessary for him to spend some months in Paris doing research. He had easily persuaded her to accompany him. She badly needed a rest from her own work and the temptation to be with him in her favorite city had been too strong to resist. This is what she told her agent in Toronto and friends back home in Montréal. The reasons she offered were true enough, as far as they went; but Claire had other hopes for the trip which she kept to herself.

Her secret assignment in this city, which held so much of the past she and Dolly shared, was to make sense of the unreasonable fears that now beset her.

Her panic had surfaced suddenly during a simple routine assignment. She had been asked to photograph a famous tycoon, the head of an international media conglomerate, based in Toronto. As soon as she arrived at his penthouse office, she realized that the setting presented problems. For one thing, the constant interruptions — telephone calls, faxes, aides requiring signatures — made it impossible for him to concentrate on the sitting. "I'll be with you in a minute," he kept assuring Claire while she waited, feeling increasingly trapped and lightheaded.

She had never felt comfortable inside these sealed towers with their artificially controlled climate — she insisted on hotel rooms where she could open a window — but dislike suddenly gave way to heart-pounding, palm-sweating terror. She no longer cared about the interruptions, or her assistant waiting for instructions on where to set up the lights, or the tycoon who kept flashing smiles at her to indicate he had not forgotten her presence. The only thing that mattered was her desperate need to get out of the room and out of the building; otherwise, she was certain she would die. Her flight seemed to take forever, turning into a slow-motion sequence as she floated past the startled faces of the people witnessing her escape. At last she was outside, still weak, clinging to the walls for support, but gulping real air. Nothing on earth could have made her go back inside the sealed capsule of a building to complete her work.

Her agent, the kinetic Lucinda Fraser, who had known Claire for years and took much credit for her success, did her best to repair the damage. Lucinda's able effort prompted the tycoon to send flowers and a note expressing the hope that Claire was feeling better. When Claire called to thank her, Lucinda told Claire she must get rid of her negative energy. "Come for a week to my ashram," she suggested, "it will do you a world of good. I don't know how I managed to get along before I found the place. I feel totally renewed after each stay." Claire, who was fond of Lucinda, refrained from reminding her that she had attributed similar restorative powers to rides on her Harley, until an injury sidelined her.

In any case, Claire wanted to forget the incident. Frightening as it had been, she preferred to think of it as an embarrassing but isolated aberration. She could not believe that the good fortune she had always enjoyed in her work would now desert her.

Her first lucky break came when she was still at college, working for the school paper. The editor, a former boyfriend, had asked her to photograph a band of armed Mohawks defending their traditional burial ground against a proposed golf course. She drove out to the disputed terrain and found herself in the right place at the right time. The site had been surrounded by police, but she succeeded in penetrating the encampment to emerge a week later with rolls of film sought after by newspapers and magazines around the world. She had been taken on by Lucinda's agency after graduating and had worked steadily since. Surely, a few bizarre symptoms could not keep her from an activity so central to her life, she reasoned.

When the symptoms recurred on two other occasions weeks apart and in circumstances seemingly unrelated, she became truly alarmed. She had always enjoyed remarkably good health and did not even have a family physician. It was Adrian who urged her to seek a consultation with his doctor, a longtime friend. Adrian's concern convinced her she could not continue to dismiss the disturbing episodes as freak occurrences.

Dr. Susan Alvarez examined Claire thoroughly, confirmed her robust constitution, and informed her she was suffering from panic attacks — a common anxiety disorder, highly amenable to treatment. She suggested that Claire follow a course in relaxation techniques and contemplate a long holiday. "That trip of Adrian's to France could not come at a better time," she told Claire. "I suspect it will do you more good than any medication I can prescribe."

Adrian was relieved by the diagnosis and encouraged Claire to follow Dr. Alvarez's advice, but Claire had her doubts: Lying on her bed, listening to the soothing voice on tape instructing her to concentrate on her breathing while she clenched and relaxed various muscles in her body, she felt anything but relieved. It seemed highly unlikely that the simple, gentle exercises she was practicing would stave off the violent responses she had experienced. More worrisome still was the nagging thought that there was something inevitable, even congenital, about her attacks. Hadn't Dolly, a talented sculptor with a promising future, abandoned her work for reasons no one had ever understood? Was she doomed to repeat her mother's aborted career? She would keep on with her relaxation exercises, but she was convinced her future depended on understanding what had happened to her mother.

This was to be her Paris quest, Claire decided, shading the word with irony, yet feeling it suited the task before her: Why had Dolly forsaken her work following her final stay in France? What had happened to change her from an ambitious artist to a sad, idle woman? The mysterious transformation occurred when Claire was thirteen and its significance grew darker with the passing years. Her search would not be easy. The truth about Dolly, she suspected, lay buried beneath years of concealment. The elegant city now appeared as a labyrinth of tantalizing pathways drawing her towards the past.

Claire was twelve when her mother won an award permitting her to work in Paris for a year. Dolly assumed her daughter would come with her, but Claire had refused. How could Dolly ask her to miss the beginning of high school when she and her friends had been talking of nothing else for months? Claire would not even listen when Dolly tried to make her see what a wonderful opportunity this was for both of them. On some level she was punishing Dolly, saying to her, if you choose your art you can't have me. The fierce struggle between them raged for weeks. By comparison, the exchanges between her parents sounded surprisingly muted to Claire as she lay in bed, listening to the murmur of their voices across the hall. Her father detested arguments.

Claire did not regret her decision. Living with her father made her feel wonderfully grown-up. His law practice kept him away from home until late in the day, and in the evening he usually read briefs or listened to music. They got on well without saying much. Have a good day? he would ask, and her brief answers sufficed without further questions. She did not feel the need to test him as she did with Dolly. She accepted his love calmly, never having cause to doubt it.

Claire scarcely missed her mother during the months she was away. Lying in bed at night, with Dolly's pastel landscapes on the walls of her bedroom, her mind raced with thoughts of school, friends and the first stirrings of adolescence. But sometimes she became angry with Dolly for the most trivial of reasons: why wasn't she around to help her find the sweater she wanted to wear, or to share her enthusiasm in a new school project?

This period coincided with her discovery of photography. Dolly had given her a camera before she left for France, saying, "I don't expect you will write much, so you can send me pictures instead. Anything that catches your eye." After a few tentative attempts — snapshots of her friends and the family cat — Claire joined the school photography club and became more confident with the camera. She photographed the pattern of morning light on her wallpaper, her father sleeping in his favorite chair, her friend's face when talking on the telephone to a boy she liked, a neighbor's child dressed in Halloween finery. Dolly sent encouraging letters, praising the results.

When Dolly returned abruptly months before her grant expired, Claire was surprised to find how thrilled she was to have her mother back. It became quickly apparent, however, that something was terribly wrong with Dolly. It was as if some other person, an impostor who resembled her mother, had returned to play the part, and played it badly.

Who was this sad, weary-looking woman who spent hours sitting idly staring into space? Claire desperately longed for the old Dolly. She had resented the time Dolly had devoted to her art, but this new Dolly seemed far more inaccessible. Weeks went by and the door to the studio remained closed. Even the countryside, where she had found such pleasure in the past, now held no interest for her.

Claire had looked to her father for an explanation, but he seemed as much at a loss as she was. "Your mother is a strong woman," he said, placing a comforting hand on her shoulder. "She'll be all right."

Claire remained unsatisfied and drew her own conclusions. Something awful must have happened to Dolly during her stay in Paris; nothing else made sense. If only she had done as her mother wished and accompanied her, she might have kept her from harm. Guilt and suspicion lingered over the years, taking root despite the absence of any real evidence.

So far, Claire had few clues to work with. She looked for answers among old family photographs, concentrating on those taken by her father during the last months of Dolly's life. The longer she examined the photographs, the more her mother's face became that of a stranger. Whatever dark secret she had carried within her remained hidden from the camera's probing eye. Claire found that these images exerted a strange hold upon her. More than the thousands of photographs taken during the course of her work, these amateur snapshots of her mother were mysteriously compelling. She returned to them again and again.

The enigmatic nature of these images suggested her mother's last works — barely delineated forms struggling to emerge from large blocks of wood. She salvaged the sculptures and stored them in a warehouse when her father sold the family home. Claire could not help feeling a sense of loss whenever she came to look at these half-formed figures, trapped forever by the artist's desertion. Who were they and what would they have become? she wondered. She thought of them as her half-brothers and sisters, orphaned like herself by Dolly's untimely death.

Reading Rousseau was another way back to Dolly. Her first attempts, instigated by Dolly years ago, had ended in boredom. Now, as she worked her way through the layers of meaning in Rousseau's writing, burrowing for a way into Dolly's mind, she regretted her earlier stubbornness. Her newfound interest in Rousseau brought her pleasure but no answers. The philosopher, she suspected, belonged to an earlier period in her mother's life, when she would return from trips to the countryside, her face glowing, her tangled hair smelling of the outdoors, her entire being filled with a kind of triumphant energy that swept Claire and her quiet father along in its path. In the end, Claire suspected, Rousseau had failed her as well.

These were the elements Claire worked with — the mysterious woman in the photographs, the barely discernible shapes emerging from blocks of wood, Rousseau's shadowy presence, and troubling memories of the sad woman who returned from Paris so changed, she scarcely resembled the mother Claire had known.

Now that she herself was in Paris, the search offered more promise. She had wandered the city, trying to imagine her mother walking the same streets. It wasn't hard. At thirty-seven, Claire was only a few years younger than Dolly had been at the time. The two women looked alike, according to the photographs Claire had seen. Even her father had noticed the resemblance the last time she had visited him in Victoria where he now lived with his new wife. They had the same dark curly hair, the same high cheekbones, broad forehead and clear gray eyes. Only Claire was taller, inheriting her height from her father's side of the family.

The relatively unchanging nature of many Paris neighborhoods enhanced the sense of continuity and intimacy with her mother's presence. Dolly had always claimed that the French brought a special kind of poetry to the ordinary acts of everyday life. Claire was happy to discover she shared her mother's sentiment. Her daily round of visits to the outdoor market, the corner bakery, the neighborhood café, the newsstand, the *traiteur* and the *marchand de vin* were all marked by courtesy and graceful banter which gave pleasure to the most ordinary of errands. It was easy to imagine her young exuberant mother beside her, guiding and encouraging her as she had done on that day long ago when Claire had learned to sail her miniature boat.

TWO

The park was beginning to empty as people headed off to lunch. Claire checked her watch to see how late Adrian was: late enough to be in serious trouble. She checked the place where they had arranged to meet, saw no sign of him, and walked on. She chose an obscure path leading towards a ravine. If Adrian had trouble finding her, he deserved no less. Playing hide-and-seek at your age, she reproached herself half-heartedly.

One of the surprising revelations of marriage, she had discovered, was that her love for Adrian did not prevent her from finding him maddeningly irritating at times. Claire's previous relationships had usually ended when irritation made its presence known. Adrian was for keeps, she was certain of that, yet lately she often felt out of sorts with him. It wasn't just his tardiness, or his penchant for abstract theorizing, or even his complacent acceptance of Marcel's flattery. It seemed to her they were out of step as never before.

She suspected it had something to do with finding herself at loose ends; too much time to dwell on troubling thoughts. The panic episodes had shaken her badly and her probing of the past was proving painful. She needed Adrian, but Adrian, embarking on a new book, seemed to have little time or interest in anything else.

Perhaps the harmony they had enjoyed in the past depended on a certain amount of separation. She thought wistfully of the eager embraces that once awaited her whenever she returned from an assignment. Now his responses painfully reminded Claire of the times she had ventured into her mother's studio as a child and felt Dolly's impatience to return to her work. Was that why she had chosen Adrian, to recapture that early experience of intense love undercut by distraction? Life was rarely that neat, she realized, but the similarity troubled her.

Fortunately, Adrian caught up with her just as her brooding threatened to excavate a new layer of distress. Her pleasure in seeing him waned when she saw Marcel trailing behind. She had been looking forward to being alone with Adrian, and Marcel was the worst person he could have chosen to bring along.

"I was worried about you," Adrian said, embracing her. "Why did you wander off?"

The embrace did not soften her heart. The petty chronic crimes of the people we live with are the hardest to forgive, Claire decided. "I got tired of waiting. You're lucky I didn't leave the park."

"I'm sorry," he said, managing to sound genuinely penitent. "The session just seemed to go on and on."

Claire forgave him. It was easier to be angry with Adrian when she was not near him. "Can we talk about this over lunch?" she said, matching his friendly tone. "I'm starving."

"Great," he said, "I have a treat for you. We stopped to book a table at the restaurant here, the Pavillon du Lac. Marcel says it's excellent. We just have to wait a little while."

"How long?" The sun had disappeared and she was feeling chilled. It did not help matters to hear Marcel say, "Impatience spoils all pleasure, my dear Claire. Come, we'll sit here for a few minutes and I promise the wait will be worthwhile."

Marcel brought out the worst in her, she decided, suppressing a sudden urge to hit him. Oblivious, he leaned over and whispered, "Adrian was absolutely brilliant this morning, the students would not let him leave. You must be so proud of him."

Claire turned away, indicating that she was not interested in pursuing conversation at the moment. Marcel gave his attention to Adrian and the two resumed their discussion about gardens. Adrian was currently working on a history of the great French gardens of the seventeenth and eighteenth centuries — Fontainebleau, Chenonceaux, Chantilly, the

Tuileries, Vaux-le-Vicomte, Versailles. It was his belief that these gardens were among the most ambitious works of art ever created and he proposed to examine the circumstances which had permitted them to flourish.

"French thinking is so rigid when it comes to gardens," he said turning to Marcel. "You insist the Anglo-Saxon view of nature is sentimental and idyllic, whereas the formal French garden is the ultimate expression of a rational spirit."

"You misunderstand us, Adrian. What you call rigidity is simply a need to classify, to establish categories. I agree that the formal French garden represents a subjugation of nature and a glorification of the human presence. All I'm suggesting is that if the seventeenth-century garden epitomized the spatial order of its time, those rules are worth examining. In this particular context, I believe, artificiality need not be an invidious word."

Claire no longer looked at gardens casually or with an eye to simple pleasures. Adrian had introduced her to a rich and varied field of study which had nothing to do with her own domestic notions about gardens, defined as they were by spring catalogues, perennial beds, and composting. Adrian, it had surprised her to learn, cared little about plants and flower beds and he was not particularly susceptible to the lure of nature, however magnificent its display. Nature assumed interest for Adrian only when it bore the imprint of an esthetic vision which transformed it into a work of art, worthy of serious consideration. She felt flattered by Adrian's eagerness to share his ideas with her. But much as she loved seeing his face come alive at such times, his passion remained abstract for her; she found herself watching the play of emotion on his face instead of listening.

Adrian's lack of interest in conventional gardening proved to be a blessing when Claire came to live with him. It had made sense for her to give up her flat and move into Adrian's spacious Victorian house. The house offered views

Claire loved of the mountain in the center of the city and the broad river flowing past its historic core. She found it difficult at first to assert her presence in its orderly interiors: they seemed to forbid the comfortable clutter that followed in her wake wherever she lived. Even her clothes, with their jumble of colors and fabrics, struck a discordant note against Adrian's sober, sparse wardrobe.

Since leaving home, Claire had lived in a succession of small, messy flats resembling each other in their careless decor and their lack of domestic amenities. Her darkroom had been the only place where a sense of order prevailed. And so, for the first few months, she had not been able to get over the feeling of being a visitor in Adrian's house. What would be the point of fussing with the interiors when they already worked so well, according to Adrian's careful design?

Then, when spring came, she discovered the garden behind the house — neglected, overgrown, beyond the pale of Adrian's interests. She claimed it as her own, learning as she went along. As she struggled with the alien vegetation, Claire wished she had paid closer attention to Dolly when she worked her magic in their garden at home. Dolly's garden had consisted mostly of wildflowers, a wonderful, curving expanse of changing color, filled with specimens she collected on her excursions into the countryside and lovingly revived. How different it had looked from the neat flowerbeds bordering their neighbors' lawns!

Claire eventually found her own way as well. By the third summer, she had transformed the tangled wilderness into an oasis of scent, color and form that she was proud to display. Slowly, the garden insinuated its presence inside the house, subtly altering it with the lushness of its offerings. As a steady procession of cut flowers — irises, delphiniums, lupines, roses, lilies and dahlias — moved indoors from early spring until late fall, Claire felt she had finally taken possession of the house.

She checked on the conversation between Adrian and Marcel, and it still failed to hold her interest. Happily, a scene of suspense developing nearby, the suspense as wonderfully contrived as the artificial cliffs behind her, caught her eye. A solemn-looking little girl, holding a large doll, warily contemplated crossing a narrow stream across a path of boulders serving as steppingstones. She attempted the first boulder and hesitated. The stones were so close and the water so shallow that the child was in no more danger than if she had been playing in her bathtub. Yet the woman accompanying the little girl — too old to be her mother — kept up a stream of warnings: "Careful Manon, take care not to slip, not too fast, now." By encouraging the child's natural timidity, she had turned the crossing into a dangerous adventure. Tension showed in the child's small face and Claire held her breath until the child had made it safely to solid ground.

It had happened again, she realized, as soon as the drama ended. Too often lately, she caught herself watching children with unusual curiosity. Did this mean she was yearning for a child, after all? Adrian, the father of fourteen-year-old Melissa, his daughter from his previous marriage, had made it clear at the outset that he did not want another child. "I'll be fifty in two years. Too old and too set in my ways to get into the baby business again." She had accepted his decision at the time and concentrated on winning Melissa over during her frequent visits with her father.

It had taken months for Melissa to soften to Claire. It might have taken forever if Claire had not cleverly used her camera as a lure. No young girl, she was certain, could resist a steady flow of flattering photographs, often taken without her knowledge. They were on their way to becoming friends now. Melissa even passed on a compliment from her mother, who requested prints of the photographs she admired.

Melissa's mother was the impeccable and glamorous Pamela Porter. At least that is how she appeared on her daily television show, which Claire could not resist watching from time to time when she worked at home. She called it her Pamela break. Sipping coffee while she observed Pamela expertly charming her guests, Claire could not believe that the Adrian she knew, sober and studious, had been married to this flamboyant woman.

"She was different before television," was all he offered when pressed for an explanation.

Still, no matter what his feelings were for the new Pamela, Claire understood that he would always be intricately linked to her through their child. By her very existence Melissa tied Adrian to his ex-wife in ways she and Adrian did not share.

Adrian's unwillingness to have another child had not troubled Claire greatly at first. Unlike some of her friends, she did not feel crazed by the thought that her chances for motherhood diminished with each passing day. Life was about choices and she had not regretted the ones she had made.

But she was no longer certain that she agreed with Adrian. She found herself questioning his reluctance to have a child with her and wondering how she really felt about it. To find out, she needed to separate her own wishes from his. Her newfound fascination with children was surely significant. While in the past, she had looked at parents and children with a distant curiosity, now she was behaving like a nervous understudy, wondering if she could master the adult role.

Her experience was limited. Her own childhood had ended abruptly the day Dolly died in a car accident, only months after her return from Paris. It happened on a blustery Montréal winter evening. Dolly was only blocks from home when a city bus, derouted by an icy patch, slid into the path of her oncoming car, sending it crashing into a tree. The policeman who had come to the house to break the news had drawn a diagram of the course followed by the two vehicles just prior to the moment of fatal collision. He also volunteered the precise time of the accident, deciphered from the smashed clock in the car.

Claire had tried hard in the days that followed to pinpoint her own actions at the time of the collision. It seemed very important to know what she had been doing. As well as she could figure it, she had been in the kitchen, dipping the ink-stained cuff of her blouse into a bowl of milk, as she had seen her mother do, watching the stain lighten with each immersion. Nearby, her father listened to the evening news. It had been a quiet, ordinary moment of no particular portent. This juxtaposition of images troubled her, or rather the truth it revealed troubled her: that people suffered and died while others, even those dear to them, listened to the radio, day-dreamed, and wondered what they would have for dinner.

In later years, she often thought of that moment, seeing herself in the quiet, neat kitchen, safe and warm on a stormy winter night, her thoughts as innocent of distress as her shirt sleeve of its former ink blemish. But she avoided thinking about Dolly, relegating her instead to a dim corner of memory which she entered only inadvertently.

Dolly's banishment appeared to be over now. Claire's fear of inheriting from her mother some fatal character flaw had brought her back to Paris, the scene of the crime, where something had killed Dolly's spirit long before the wayward bus crushed her body on an icy Montréal road.

She stood up, making an effort to shake off her morbid thoughts. Turning to the men, she said, "I'm going in. Ready or not, they will have to feed me. Otherwise, I shall make a dreadful scene."

"Beware of Claire when she's really hungry," Adrian said, joining her. "There's no telling what she will do." Marcel still hesitated, but Adrian pulled him to his feet and he followed them obediently.

THREE

Their table was waiting when they arrived at the Pavillon du Lac, a pretty, white art deco building with tall windows giving on to the lake. Once seated and the food ordered, waiters surrounded them, moving gracefully back and forth, performing the rites of the table. Each course of the *menu du jour* arrived modestly concealed inside domes of silver, china or canopies of greenery, only to be revealed dramatically by the waiters in a sort of Epicurean Dance of the Seven Veils.

They began with a simple and delicious Cavaillon melon infused with port wine, then a *bar au fenouil* in lace-like pastry, followed by an aspic of goose liver and truffles, then slivers of lamb resting on a bed of chanterelle mushrooms, then a taste of cheese, *le brie des Meaux*, and finally delicate crêpes filled with wild strawberries. The small portions, reminding Claire of a children's tea party, prevented the usual ill effects of overindulgence, despite the elaborate menu. Watching Marcel partake of the food while continuing to expound his theories, each activity producing its own measure of ecstasy on his flushed face, Claire considered her dislike of him.

He had met them at the airport when they had arrived and it seemed to her he had not left their side since. He had appeared, on that occasion, carrying a copy of an art history journal with Adrian's photograph (taken by Claire) on the cover and Marcel's flattering account of Adrian's work inside. During the long taxi ride into Paris, he had ignored Claire to concentrate on Adrian. Whenever they met at his café, Marcel praised Adrian's work to acquaintances who stopped by their table, and failed to introduce Claire. Adrian assured her that Marcel's behavior was due to his awkwardness with women, not rudeness.

27

Adrian's tolerance of Marcel was no doubt due to Marcel's admiration for him, which knew no bounds. When they were with other people and Adrian held the floor, he could not restrain himself at times from whispering in Claire's ear, *"Quel bel homme.* He has the profile of a Roman statue." Claire sometimes caught Marcel looking at her with an expression of bewilderment, as if he were trying to understand why she was the one Adrian chose to take home and not him. It did not help matters that Adrian accepted Marcel's slavish adoration with easy complacence.

Claire couldn't decide which she disliked more, the times when Marcel behaved as if she were invisible, or the rarer occasions when he made an effort to talk to her, usually about photography, displaying as always his impressive erudition. His notice of her, Claire suspected, arose from a desire to please Adrian, as if by tossing a sliver of attention her way, he hoped to forestall any restlessness which would distract Adrian from his own words.

She had thought Marcel a snob until she saw how lavishly he extended his wit and erudition to everyone who crossed his path: taxi drivers, bus conductors, waiters, the woman in the flower shop, his *concièrge*, the regulars in the café where he took care of his appointments. (His own apartment was so crammed with books, there was no room to entertain visitors.) In a society where agility with words was as highly valued as dexterity with a soccer ball, his talents were greeted with affection and admiration. She seemed to be alone in disliking him.

Claire complained about Marcel to Zoé Lagarde, who was her closest friend in Paris from her student days. Zoé, a respected psychoanalyst, suggested that his behavior was due more to ineptness than hostility. She suspected some form of anxiety neurosis. Claire trusted Zoé's judgement. She began to notice that Marcel, a large unkempt man in his mid-forties, was always at the mercy of one ailment or another. Since their arrival, he had suffered a variety of flu-like symptoms, an abscessed tooth had distended his cheek, an attack of gout had forced him to hobble, and he was frequently obliged to resort to an inhalator to relieve his shallow, asthmatic breathing. These afflictions, never borne stoically, usually required the assistance of friends, students, his ex-wife, all enlisted in the cause of alleviating Marcel's suffering.

Zoé was right, Claire decided, spooning the last of the delicious dessert into her mouth. She watched Marcel struggling to balance his passions for food and words, each mouthful or *bon mot* punctuated by a childlike smile of self-satisfaction. She had to admit he was more comical than anything. So was she for that matter, playing the jealous wife, a role she could not sustain for very long. The good food and the wine encouraged a more benign view of events. When Marcel proposed an outing for the following weekend to the park at Ermenonville, she offered no objections.

"The gardens at Ermenonville were inspired by Rousseau," he explained for her benefit. "I will be staying nearby with friends. Come on Sunday. We'll have an early lunch and visit the gardens in the afternoon. I'll arrange everything."

Adrian, sensing her change of mood, took her hand beneath the tablecloth and gave it a little squeeze, as if to say, "you and I are connected no matter what goes on around us." She glanced at his face, which looked a little dazed from the wine and the onslaught of Marcel's monologue, and her heart filled with affection. How lucky they were to have found each other.

Adrian and Claire's affection had blossomed under the beneficent sign of unexpected good fortune, which they attributed to their initial meeting.

Claire had been commissioned to photograph Adrian Arensberg for the cover of his new book, *The Itinerant Eye — the Esthetics of Scenery*. Eclectic in scope and sweeping in its use of learned sources, it became one of those rare books, intended for a specialized audience, which succeed in leaping across the barrier between respectable obscurity and celebrity to sell in astonishingly large numbers.

Adrian insisted that meeting Claire was the best thing that had happened to him in years. Claire, weary of failure and longing, had nearly given up thinking of herself as a person who would marry. She had responded to Adrian's ardor with caution, suspicious of the intensity of their feelings — she had been there before — until she could no longer resist his certainty. Slowly, she had learned to trust his soundness and his generous spirit. The acceptance she saw in his eyes at all times awakened her own kindness. She forgave his fits of abstraction, seeing them as a sign of devotion to his work — the same devotion he lavished on her and Melissa when the work was set aside.

Once, soon after they met, Adrian took her to a reception for a celebrated Italian art historian who was to speak at the university where Adrian taught. He warned her to expect a dull faculty evening. The guest of honor was in the middle of the room when they arrived, surrounded by admiring faculty members and a few graduate students. As they drew nearer, the circle of admirers suddenly opened and widened, as if they were children playing farmer-in-the-dell, to reveal the visitor alone in the center, a freshly lit cigarette in his hand. Unaware of prevailing feelings against smoking and the absence of ashtrays, he looked a little startled by the effect he had produced.

It was then that Adrian did something wonderful. Although he himself did not smoke and disliked being near people who did, Adrian walked over to the visitor and asked for a cigarette. Then, taking his arm, he led him onto the terrace off the reception room. Watching the two men from inside where the conversation had nervously resumed, Claire felt that she had never seen anyone demonstrate greater delicacy of feeling for others. How could she have resisted him?

They decided to walk off the lunch and head for the Gustave-Moreau Museum, one of Adrian's favorite places. Marcel, of course, accompanied them.

They walked slowly through tight, narrow streets, past shuttered stores and crowded cafés. The midday pause was still being observed. Turning the corner into a narrow medieval street, Adrian drew her attention to an ornate gateway that interrupted the street's austere appearance. The doors were ajar and they ventured inside to discover a peaceful, rural scene, with tall poplars defining narrow, unpaved pathways where elaborately carved tombstones followed each other in neighborly proximity.

This was the kind of place to which she was instantly drawn. Whenever Claire traveled, she kept a sharp lookout for such small enclaves of serenity, hidden patches of resistance amid the swirl of big city energy. She reached for one of the two small Minox cameras she kept in her shoulder bag. Before she could even focus, she heard someone shouting, "*Arrêtez, arrêtez.* No pictures allowed."

A small, round man, with a table napkin still tucked inside his shirt collar, was rushing towards her, waving his arms in case she had missed his words.

"I see no signs forbidding photographs," Claire responded, familiar with the protocol for such occasions.

"But yes, *Mademoiselle.* Right here," he said with cheerful insistence, pointing Claire in the direction of a long, printed scroll attached to the caretaker's gatehouse. "If you will permit me . . ." he said, bowing politely before disappearing inside.

"Forget it, Claire," Adrian said. "He's probably right. The French have so many rules proscribing all variety of behavior in public places, no official has any need to invent."

But she was stubbornly committed to finding the interdiction in writing. She skimmed through the long list of acts forbidden within the confines of the cemetery until she spotted the appropriate phrase relating to her illicit activity.

The caretaker had now reemerged from the gatehouse, resplendent in his official uniform, decorated with gold braid and brass buttons. "You have found it?" he asked Claire with an encouraging smile which turned to a broad beam of approval when she nodded.

Claire found herself returning his smile. In her younger days she would have been indignant in the face of such complacent authority. Now, Claire noted the well-kept, pleasant grounds and appreciated the caretaker's pride in performing his duties. She could see him removing the glittering uniform before he headed for lunch across the street. There, seated at his usual table near the window, from which he could survey his domain, he had seen strangers enter his precinct. Without hesitation, he had abandoned his meal and rushed to his post. If anything, Claire felt she had been guilty of a lack of consideration by coming at such an inconvenient time and disturbing his meal.

"If you like," Marcel offered after the custodian had ushered them out with a courtly "*à votre service*," "I can probably arrange for permission to allow you to photograph. It wouldn't take more than a week or so."

"Thank you Marcel, it was only a whim." He was probably trying to ingratiate himself with Adrian again, Claire suspected. It would spoil her pleasure the next time she chose to be angry with him if she accepted his help.

They walked on in silence, the gentle torpor of the afternoon slowing their steps as they climbed rue de la Rochefoucault. "This is it," Adrian announced, stopping in front of an elegant gray stone *hôtel particulier*, indistinguishable from its solid neighbors on the gently sloping street. The French symbolist painter, Gustave Moreau, had lived here, he explained, first with his parents and later alone until his death in 1898. They had the place to themselves, they discovered, as they explored the grand reception rooms and the soaring double-height studio filled with the artist's works.

Claire lacked Adrian's ability to lose himself in the contemplation of a single work of art, and she soon wandered off on her own. She made her way up the curving spiral staircase to the upper half of the atelier. A woman about her own age and a small child were the only other visitors.

Claire sat down on a leather seat in the middle of the room to rest for a moment. She felt squashed by the enormous canvas facing her, as if she were sitting in a movie theater too close to the screen. It portrayed two winged, armed figures rising in a frozen blue sky while below the damned city perished by fire. She checked and saw that it was called "The Angels of Sodom."

Were cities always associated with corruption, or were the angels having their own version of a panic attack? she wondered, looking at the canvas. She was becoming something of an expert in spotting the syndrome.

A persistent clicking sound interrupted her thoughts. She looked around for its source and saw the child — a little girl — trying to turn a revolving display of drawings encased in metal frames. The mother stood behind the little girl, helping her move the frames. The child appeared to be more interested in the mechanics of the display and the sound made by the frames crashing into each other than in the drawings themselves. The mother tried to minimize the noise with a restraining hand, talking to the child in a soft, patient voice.

Claire could not hear the mother's words, but the scene was familiar. On Sundays and holidays she had often accompanied Dolly to museums. While Dolly looked at art, Claire had quietly amused herself as she liked. She had found allies among the bored museum guards. On a memorable occasion, one had offered her candy. Dolly's sporadic attempts to make her see the wonder of some specific work usually ended in frustration. Claire distrusted Dolly's enthusiasm and stubbornly refused to share it.

33

"Do you want to see my purse?" The little girl stood in front of her holding open a small patent leather shoulder bag.

Before Claire had a chance to reply, the child's mother whisked her away. "You must not bother people," she admonished. "They come here to look at paintings, not to chat with naughty little girls."

Claire wanted to tell the mother that she was actually more interested in the child than in the paintings, but she was prevented by Adrian's entrance.

She knew Adrian had seen her talking to the child, and the tightness around his mouth told her the scene made him uneasy. She could have put his mind at ease by telling him she had been thinking of the past and not the present, but she said nothing. It did not displease her to have him believe she had been brooding about the baby business, as he called it. Every marriage, she was beginning to see, even the best of marriages, produced its inevitable crop of resentments and reprisals.

FOUR

The next day Claire decided to visit Dolly's childhood friend, Marta. She had grown up with Marta's presence, evoked by Dolly in the stories she told her daughter. Claire's favorite was the one in which Marta appeared unexpectedly at the foot of her cradle — an unannounced visit to surprise her friend and lend a hand with the new baby — a fairy god mother who swaddled her in her first Parisian finery.

In person, Marta Berkmann turned out to be brusque and intimidating. During her student year in Paris, Claire often found herself dreading Sunday dinners at Marta's. Marta's criticism of Claire — her long, wild hair and her lackadaisical efforts to get to know the city were frequent targets — would make her blush with embarrassment. Marta's husband, Bruno, always came to Claire's defense, forestalling the tears provoked by his wife.

Marta was still difficult, still unpredictable, but no longer intimidating. Claire now knew that Marta loved her both for herself and for being Dolly's daughter. She and Marta had come to appreciate one another in ways that had not been possible when Claire was younger and less confident.

Claire counted on Marta to help her solve the mystery of Dolly's unhappy transformation. So far, she had learned nothing. Despite her efforts to steer the conversation toward the subject of Dolly whenever she and Marta were together, Marta invariably managed to veer off in other directions.

It was true she had a great deal on her mind. Marta's relationship with Henri, her companion since Bruno's death eight years earlier, threatened to deteriorate as Henri pressed her to give up her flat and move in with him. There was Marta's ongoing dispute with the tax people concerning her earnings from translation work she had done for an American advertising firm. And most of all, Marta worried about her grandson, Antoine, who lacked any sense of direction and whose parents, Marta's daughter and son-in-law, failed to provide proper guidance, according to Marta.

Marta's ongoing tribulations forced Claire to suppress her own questions. She was not someone who normally measured her words or hesitated to ask questions, but Marta's ingenious ways of involving Claire in her crises stymied her. Claire was forced to wait for the right moment. It might never come, she was beginning to realize, unless she resorted to a little verbal bullying.

Claire was disappointed to find Henri with Marta when she arrived at Marta's flat. She had hoped to have Marta to herself and compel her to talk about Dolly. Marta seemed anxious for Henri to leave as well. Claire sensed that she had walked in on one of their frequent quarrels. She knew Marta well enough to recognize that her distracted manner and the excessive brightness in her grayish-blue eyes were due to agitation.

"Hello darling," she said, kissing Claire in an abstracted way. Henri, a shy, reserved man, greeted her with a formal handshake and downcast eyes. His smooth face and contrite expression gave him the uneasy look of a child who has just been severely scolded.

Before she could assess the situation further, the telephone rang. She would really have to get Marta out of the house, she thought, if she hoped to have a proper conversation with her. Marta seemed to be at the heart of a circle of foreigners — political exiles, expatriates — whose abilities to cope with old age and the intricacies of French bureaucracy were less adequate than her own. Some had never learned the language properly; others lived on small, fixed incomes from abroad and were struggling to survive in a city that had changed from an inexpensive haven for foreigners to a place notorious for its high cost of living. It sounded at times as if Marta was running a social service agency on behalf of her friends.

"It's Gertrude," she whispered, and Claire's heart sank. Marta's conversations with her friend Gertrude tended to go on forever. Not this time, however. "Her problems will keep," Marta said, after hanging up. " They're always the same — a tale of unending endurance — I told you her husband suffers from Alzheimer's. Really, I don't know how she goes on. She has been a good friend to me over the years, but it's all I can do just to visit her. Let's not talk of sad things. Tell me, what have you been up to?"

Marta liked to have a full report of Claire and Adrian's daily activities. She had lived in Paris for nearly fifty years now, and despite the new buildings she deplored — "I prefer old stones," she confided to Claire and Adrian — her passion for the city remained undiminished. According to Marta, those unfortunate enough to live elsewhere should make the most of their limited time in the City of Light by applying themselves to a rigorous study of its treasures.

"It's not enough to pick up a travel guide and tick off the principal monuments one by one," Marta asserted. "You need to see all of Paris as a museum. The customs of ordinary life reveal as much about the character of Paris as its famous landmarks."

Claire dutifully reported the highlights of the day, wondering why Marta's approval still mattered. When she mentioned the Gustave-Moreau Museum, Marta responded with enthusiasm. "Your Adrian knows the city better than most Parisians. Henri, on the other hand, insists there is nothing left to see. If it were up to him, we would never leave the house." Claire realized Marta was not ready to abandon her quarrel with Henri.

Henri stirred uncomfortably in his chair, apparently sensing where Marta was headed.

"I don't know what makes her say that," he protested without much conviction. Henri adored Marta and admired the energy and passion with which she tackled life, including her attempts to force him out of his placid widower's existence. He did not understand her moods, but he gratefully offered her his phlegmatic temperament as a foil for her outbursts. "Why Marta, we've been out all morning."

"Can you believe this man?" Marta said, responding on cue. "I had to drag him out to buy a new sports jacket. He has some crazy notion that at his age he no longer needs new clothes. I reminded him that he can be as abstemious as he likes in the grave, but here, above ground, life demands its decorum. In any case, I hardly call that an outing. Now, he feels he has to rest for the remainder of the day."

"You exaggerate, Marta," Henri said in a placating tone, as he rose from his chair to put on his coat. He had learned that the best thing he could do when Marta was in one of her moods was to leave; his presence only inflamed her irritation. "I'm going home to have a nap and after dinner we will go wherever you like."

As she watched him calmly put on his overcoat, carefully tucking the ends of his scarf inside it, and turning to kiss Marta without a hint of rancor, Claire couldn't help feeling sorry for him. It wasn't easy to be the object of Marta's disapproval, she well knew. Although Claire, along with everyone else in Marta's circle of intimates, considered mild, soft-spoken Henri a pale substitute for the charismatic Bruno, Marta's deceased husband, she felt compelled to defend him.

"You're too harsh with Henri, he adores you, Marta," she began.

"Please say no more," Marta replied, raising her hand in a gesture of weariness. "I tell myself that constantly." Her anger changed quickly to remorse as she continued. "I know, I know. I'm being horrible, but I can't help it. Henri has a way of coddling himself that I find irritating beyond words. The weather never quite suits him. It's too hot, too cold, too windy. Wherever we go, he finds the streets too crowded, too noisy, too dirty. He dislikes going to restaurants, movies, museums — in short, anywhere I might want to go. All he really wants out of life is to stay home with me at his side while he reads, watches television, and enjoys the meals I prepare. Believe me, it's more than I can bear at times."

Marta paused to answer another call from Gertrude and Claire marveled at her calm tone as she tried to rally her friend's spirits. She resumed her narrative without missing a beat. "I'm lucky to have him, I know. At this period in our lives, there are twenty lonely women for every available man. Much as we try to keep busy and put up a cheerful front, unwanted solitude, like gravity, causes bodies and spirits to sag. Whatever feminists say, unalleviated female company makes women's faces shrivel for reasons that have nothing to do with age. I'm afraid it's still a man's world. Henri is well-off, his mind works after a fashion, he's mobile when you can pry him off his sofa. What else does a man need to be considered a great catch in this world— *un beau parti*, as the French say?"

Claire laughed, appreciating Marta's wit, and Marta joined her. "It's good to have you here. I need someone to talk to."

Claire was flattered to find herself in the position of Marta's confidant, a privilege Marta extended to few people. She enjoyed hearing Marta's stories. The dense texture of other people's family ties was something she always found hard to resist, her own being so tenuous and threadbare. With Adrian, she felt she had won the kinship sweepstakes. Their marriage had introduced her to an ongoing serial of Arensberg family events, recounted and analyzed in endless telephone conversations between his sisters, aunts, cousins, nieces and nephews. Claire absorbed these tales with the curiosity of an anthropologist parachuted into an unknown tribe. Yet, for all their efforts to welcome her, she knew she would always remain an outsider.

"Henri insists I move in with him," Marta continued in a calmer tone. "I honestly don't think I can do it. It is nice to have a man to go to dinner with or to a concert, even if you have to coax him to get him there. But I'm always happy to find myself alone again in my apartment. I'm one of those people who needs a certain amount of solitude every day. Is that so unusual? Henri seems to think so. He feels I'm being selfish, uncaring. Perhaps he's right. I never realized how fortunate I was with Bruno, who was happy to leave me to my own devices. Too much so at times, of course. But then marriage is always an approximation, isn't it? A rough estimate of the appropriate response that, as often as not, falls wide of the mark, as you may have already discovered. God, there are days I still miss Bruno desperately."

Marta fell silent and the two women sat companionably watching the evening shadows advance across Marta's living room. The room had scarcely changed since Claire had first seen it all those years ago. The brown velour sofas and armchairs seemed a little lower now, pulled down by the weight of passing years. The bits of woven and embroidered cloth, souvenirs from Marta and Bruno's frequent travels, had faded where the white muslin curtains failed to keep out the light. The shelves of the glass-covered cabinets seemed more crowded with books, family photographs and other mementos. Only Bruno was missing. His favorite armchair, where he used to sit reading *Le Monde* and smoking while Claire and Marta chatted, still seemed to bear the imprint of his body.

"You know, Bruno in his own way was not an easy man to live with," Marta resumed. "Men devoted to a cause have little to offer their intimates. Much as I miss him, I'm still clear-eyed about the past. Yet there are times I find Henri unbearable, particularly when he is holding forth on how there are too many foreigners in Paris who are all becoming his personal financial burden. I feel as if I'm betraying everything Bruno fought for by being with a man like Henri, a decent man, who nevertheless shares the prejudices of his class."

There had been nothing about Bruno Berkmann's appearance when Claire first met him to suggest his past political zeal. A slight, reticent man, he was not given to reminiscences or any kind of self-glorification. Yet, as Claire had learned from Dolly and later from Marta, his small, spare frame concealed a steely determination. Despite his seeming frailty, he had survived violent strikes and long periods of solitary confinement. By the time Claire knew him, his militant days were over. Failing health had forced him to curtail his activities, but his convictions never softened. He continued to attack the injustices of the day in the pages of the small left-wing journal he edited and printed until his death.

In later years, on the rare occasions when he spoke publicly — Marta by then had become fierce in protecting Bruno's failing health from the demands his former comrades continued to make upon him — his full-throated speech with its Central European accent still conveyed power and magnetism. It was easy to understand how he had once enthralled crowds and moved men to dangerous actions. Claire had been stunned when she had heard Bruno speak at a May Day rally; his voice, distorted by amplifiers and unfamiliar in its resonance, seemed to direct the people around her almost at will.

With Claire, Bruno had always been gentle and affectionate, and she had taken to him from the moment she arrived in Paris. More so than to Marta, for she had sensed in Bruno a true ally. Her feelings for Bruno made her feel guilty whenever she thought of her own father, also a kind and thoughtful man. Since her mother's death, however, conversations with her father had become painfully awkward.

41

Claire sensed that her father did not want to be plagued by her questions and they soon abstained from mentioning Dolly; the subject was too hurtful to broach. This avoidance contaminated their exchanges. They lapsed into long silences interspersed with bits of stilted conversation from which they both turned away with relief. Claire had left for Paris and then attended university in another city. Her father had remarried during her absence and moved to Victoria. She knew her father loved her, despite the distance and the awkwardness — his new wife confided that he kept a scrapbook of Claire's work — yet she could not help thinking of herself as orphaned. No wonder she basked in the warmth Bruno and even Marta lavished upon her, the daughter of their dear friend.

Being with them, she felt closer to Dolly, as if the affection they extended admitted her to the tight circle that had once united Dolly, Marta and Bruno. Her father had never been part of it. Without anything specific being said, Claire understood that in many ways Dolly had been closer to Marta and Bruno than to her own husband. Her visits with them usually produced a glow of health and excitement that could not be due entirely to the treasures found in Paris museums. It was easy to evoke the old friends in this room where their young faces smiled down upon her and where the reverberation of their animated voices lingered in the air.

Thinking of Dolly reminded Claire of her purpose in coming here. "I need your help, Marta," she said, moving closer to the older woman.

She was rewarded with a look of warm affection. "Of course, darling. What's on your mind?"

"I want to know about Dolly's last visit to Paris. Anything you can remember."

"Why on earth do you want to know that?"

She could not tell Marta about her panic attacks and their disruptive effect on her work. Marta, generous and quick to help a friend with a practical problem, had little patience with failures of the spirit, seeing them as character flaws to be vanquished by disciplined effort.

"She's pre-Freudian," Zoé explained, "not unusual among old revolutionaries."

Claire preferred Marta's dismissive attitude to her agent Lucinda's efforts to be helpful. "You must figure out why you need to have panic attacks," Lucinda reiterated with irritating regularity, inspired no doubt by the wisdom she had acquired at her ashram.

"Whatever happens to us is of our own choosing," she insisted until Claire ordered her to stop. But Lucinda only withdrew temporarily. When she resumed her badgering, Claire screamed. "You're like a Jehovah's Witness. Abuse only confirms your faith." Laughter made them friends again, but Claire was glad not to be in close contact with Lucinda for a while.

Now, the look of dismay on Marta's face quickened her pulse. "I believe something happened to Dolly during her stay here. It had to be something awful because it changed her to the point where she could no longer work. You know how passionate she was about her art."

It was Marta's turn to hesitate. Finally, when Claire was about to rephrase her question, Marta said, "I don't think it was anything as melodramatic as you suggest. There may have been a pause in her work, but she had stopped before, you know. Right after you were born, for example. She had been married for some years before you arrived and she was utterly enchanted with motherhood. In one of her letters, I remember, she used the phrase 'the cow-like happiness of maternity,' to describe the way she felt after your birth. It stuck in my mind because my own reaction to my daughter's birth was one of intense relief — to be a separate, distinct person again and leave behind the messiness of pregnancy and childbirth. But then Dolly was always a sensualist. It's what made her forms so alluring. In any case, what I'm trying to say is that had she not run into that stupid bus, she would have returned to her work."

Marta's tone indicated she had exhausted the subject, but Claire was not satisfied. "You may be right about her work; we'll never know, will we? But there was more to it. I remember her being so terribly sad, as if she had suffered some great loss. I was only a kid and yet I couldn't help noticing the change in her. It was as if something had died inside her."

She had succeeded again in agitating Marta. "What an awful thing to believe. It's bad enough Dolly had to die when she did, but to imply that she was already dead is a sacrilege. As her daughter, you owe it to her not to dishonor the memory of the person she was. She was a gifted artist above everything else, not the poor, tormented wretch you describe. Don't forget, I knew her much longer than you did. She never let anything get in the way of her work. Not even you."

Marta jumped up and began tidying the room. Newspapers in hand, she turned back to glare at Claire. "Why all this sudden concern about her work? Neither you nor your father had any appreciation for her talent. In fact, you resented the time she devoted to it. So why now?"

Claire was stunned by the ferocity of Marta's attack. "I was only a child," she mumbled, trying to justify herself, but Marta cut her off. "Yes, and you still behave like one. Your so-called suspicions are nothing more than the fevered imaginings of an over-indulged, only child. I think it's indecent to speculate in this way about someone who can't answer for herself."

Claire had rarely seen Marta so angry with her. Instead of backing off, she became more convinced than ever that she was on the right track. "There's no betrayal in wanting to know what happened to someone you care about," she said carefully. She had to keep Marta talking. "Surely you understand."

"I do indeed," Marta answered fiercely. "Dolly was your mother, but she was also a person in her own right. If something happened to her, as you insist, then it belongs to her. None of us has the right to know everything about another person, no matter how much we care about them. Obsessive curiosity might be appropriate between lovers, otherwise it's indecent."

Claire's resolve wavered. She was immensely annoyed to find her eyes filling with tears. "You're saying I have no right to pry into her life?"

Marta's expression softened and she took hold of Claire's hand. "Darling, you know how much I care for you. In many ways you are closer to me than my own daughter. You're all I have left of Dolly and I see her in you whenever I look at you. I don't want to make you unhappy, but you must leave your mother's past alone. Isn't your life absorbing enough? You have interesting work, you have Adrian who, despite his preoccupation with his own work, cares a great deal about you. What's missing?"

Claire resisted the impulse to throw herself into Marta's arms and confess her problems. She knew from experience she would regret it. Marta's quota of tenderness was quickly used up and Claire could not bear her reproaches.

In the face of Claire's silence, Marta offered her own solution. "Maybe you should think about having a child before it's too late. God knows, I'm not a particularly maternal woman, but it's an experience I wouldn't have missed for anything. For one thing, it links you to the future and allows you to put your own relations with your parents to rest. You don't want to end up like so many childless people, lavishing your affection on some dumb animal."

The shot was well directed. Marta had seen the photographs Claire had taken of her calico cat. Trust Marta to hit every vulnerable target.

"Adrian and I have decided not to have children," she said, feeling she owed it to Adrian not to reveal their disagreements.

"Nonsense," Marta said, warming to the subject. "It's all right for Adrian, who already has a daughter and a large loving family, but it's different for you. You're very much alone in the world and time is not on your side. If you really wanted a child, I'm sure you could convince him. Despite what they say, any man finds it flattering when a woman announces she wants to bear his child."

"I have been thinking about it lately," Claire admitted reluctantly. "But I'm not sure the time is right."

"Not everything in life can be decided rationally, you know. Sometimes it's easier to allow yourself to be swept away by events. Before it's too late."

Claire was not happy with the way their afternoon was ending. She doubted, however, that she could get anything more out of Marta just then. "I will think about it," she said, "but you must promise that if you remember anything about Dolly's stay here, you will tell me."

Walking home, Claire thought Marta had been right about one thing: she had given in too easily to Adrian's reasoned objections. Well, she no longer felt docile. Her indignation flared at the thought of Adrian's unfairness. How dare he make decisions involving their future without taking her wishes into account! But as soon as she articulated her resentment, she recognized the problem. She didn't really know how badly she wanted a child. Sometimes she yearned for a baby the way she had once yearned for the touch of a lover; other times, the thought of turning her life upside down terrified her. Of course, thanks to the panic attacks, her life was not what it used to be. Were the attacks a trick her body was playing on her? What if Lucinda was right? In that case, what did they mean? Did she secretly want to give up work and have a baby?

Stop it, she told herself sternly, you'll drive yourself mad. Remember why you're here and concentrate on the quest. You can handle Adrian later, when you're back in Montréal. Another few months won't matter.

Turning her attention to the passing scenery along her route between Marta's flat and the studio she and Adrian rented on rue St. Antoine, she found her spirits lifting. The best thing about travel, she was again reminded, was this sharp-eyed way of seeing things, as if one's vision suddenly improved with a change of scenery.

FIVE

Claire enjoyed telling Zoé about her visit with Marta. Zoé had been listening to stories about Marta for nearly sixteen years, since the beginning of their friendship. They met during Claire's first week in Paris when Zoé came to her aid after she had locked herself out of her room. At the time, Claire had been wearing nothing but a short raincoat, her makeshift bathrobe, worn whenever she headed down the hall to the communal bathroom for her morning bath. She did not relish the prospect of descending six flights to the *concierge's* lodge in this flimsy attire to seek her help. By confessing her carelessness, she would be letting down her countrymen, she felt.

Claire decided to try her neighbor, a girl about her own age, whom she had noticed shortly after moving in. Zoé opened the door to find Claire barefoot, clutching her Burberry, her hair wrapped in a towel, and understood the situation immediately. She had taken her in, offered her a bowl of *café au lait*, and, more importantly, a hair dryer. Claire had not yet managed to purchase a two-pronged adapter that would have allowed her to use her own hair dryer, and her long, curly hair had been wildly unkempt since her arrival.

Despite the school French she had learned and used adequately in Montréal, Claire's knowledge of the language at the time had not withstood Zoé's rapid delivery and the student colloquialisms she favored. But there was no misunderstanding the immediate affinity they felt for each other. The friendship, which began that day, endured after Claire returned to North America at the end of the school year. Now, they relied on the telephone and Claire's visits; both were lazy letter writers, and Zoé avoided plane travel despite her success in treating other people's phobias. Zoé kept promising to do something about her fear, but so far, she hadn't. "I'm a homebound creature," was the lame excuse she offered when prodded by Claire.

"What a terrible example for your patients," Claire teased her. "Make an effort for their sake if not for mine."

"On the contrary. My patients appreciate my ability to empathize with them. It's my family and friends who are unsympathetic."

Fortunately, whenever Claire found herself in Paris, they easily resumed their closeness, sharing the important events that had transpired since they had last seen each other. Claire missed Zoé when they were apart, but she suspected that the special qualities she and Zoé ascribed to the friendship had much to do with the telescoping of narrative and emotion, imposed upon them by the infrequency of their meetings.

Zoé's work as a psychoanalyst obliged her to spend her days listening to people talk about their troubled lives. Yet, she assured Claire, there was nothing she liked better than to sit across the room from Claire, the two of them encased in the deep leather chairs of her living room, listening to Claire's account of her adventures.

"I lead a very dull existence," Zoé insisted. "Just look at the way I spend my days. I see my patients, whose problems, for the most part, are as familiar as the pattern of the Oriental rug under my feet, a gift from my parents. At night, when the last patient has left, there's dinner with the family, then I read, do the crossword puzzle, and soon it's time for bed. On Sundays, I visit my mother and if the weather is fine, we walk in the Luxembourg Gardens. Twice a week I play tennis with the same partner I've had for ten years. One night a week, I go to a *hammam*, the oriental baths, where I enjoy the steam room and a relaxing massage. I watch myself moving smoothly through this unvarying routine, fantasizing like a schoolgirl about other lives, even the tormented lives of my patients, and yet I never do anything out of character. Laziness or contentment? I can't decide."

Like all true friends, Claire and Zoé admired and envied each other. Claire's footloose existence seemed wonderfully exotic to Zoé: she found it unimaginable that anyone could travel as far and as often as Claire did, and survive with no ill effect.

Claire, of course, did not see Zoé's life as dull. Endless waits in interchangeable airports, for example, seemed to her far duller than Zoé's well-ordered daily routine. More than once, stuck in some anonymous hotel room, feeling lonely and unable to sleep, she pictured Zoé moving about her elegant apartment on rue des Beaux-Arts, and envied the smooth surface of her life. But Zoé laughed at such notions and insisted that only Claire's visits roused her from the gentle torpor in which she languished. Claire, in turn, found herself arranging her stories to please Zoé and fulfill her expectations of excitement and adventure.

Zoé, with her small body and her little boy's haircut, looked like a child sitting cross-legged in the oversized armchair. She laughed with delight as Claire described the latest exchange between Marta and Henri. Claire was keeping her own conversation with Marta to herself for the moment.

"They're wonderful," Zoé said, wiping her eyes. "Can you imagine, at their age? Simon and I hardly fight about anything any more. It all seems to have been settled ages ago, at least the big questions. You know, sex, money, who's responsible for what. Of course, Simon and I still get on each other's nerves occasionally. In fact, we both have become more irritable and cranky lately. Little inveterate habits have evolved into full-blown obsessions with time, but we've learned to handle our irritation with a mere look or a word. Even a sigh does the trick. You can't imagine how much weight Simon's sighs can carry. Truly, I can't remember when we last had an out-and-out brawl. I think we're too bored to fight."

Zoé's voice had turned wistful as she said this and Claire laughed. She knew Zoé exaggerated the monotonous nature of her life, still she wondered if she and Adrian would ever reach this level of resignation. Somehow, knowing her own nature, she doubted it.

"Look who I found in the entrance hall," Simon said entering the room with Adrian. Simon Lagarde, a high-ranking civil servant, wore the uniform of his profession — a well-tailored dark blue suit, striped shirt, and discreet tie. Adrian, slightly older than Simon, appeared much younger in his open-necked shirt and black leather jacket.

"Lucky I ran into him," Simon continued, crossing the room to kiss Zoé and Claire. "Adrian was all set to climb six flights until I informed him that we are now the proud possessors of an elevator. It's true only two people can use it at a time, but you have no idea what a difference it has made. Zoé and I had begun to dread the day the climb would finally prove too much for us — a day, I might add, that in my case seemed to loom closer with each year. I propose a toast to the little elevator that saved us from banishment and inevitable exile from our beloved *quartier*." Without waiting for a response, Simon prepared to open the bottle of champagne he produced from his brief-case. "I believe it's still adequately chilled," he said, pouring it into four fluted glasses.

One of the nice things about Zoé and Claire's friendship was that they liked each other's husbands. Although they tended to complain about their partners to each other, neither woman was influenced by the other's criticism. When Claire saw Simon, she never thought about his snoring, his excessive neatness, his brooding, his lack of spontaneity — items high on Zoé's list of complaints. The Simon she knew was invariably charming, well mannered, and as ebullient as the champagne he favored. Zoé, for her part, confessed to Claire more than once that she found Adrian very attractive. None of this meant anything in itself, except to make for agreeable times together.

This evening was no exception. After debating whether they should eat in or go out, Simon and Adrian went off to the local *traiteur* and came back with vast quantities of food.

"This is going to kill me," Zoé announced in a plaintive voice, wrapping her arms around her body as if to ward off a blow. The others ignored her as they unwrapped the elegant packages. Zoé always claimed she was getting fat despite evidence to the contrary. "I'm practically a midget," she protested, "an extra kilo makes an enormous difference to someone my size."

"*Oui chérie*," Simon responded, "you must only taste and leave the real eating to the rest of us normal-sized people."

"You're a beast," she said, but she was unable to resist the laughter of the others.

The men blamed one another for their extravagance, while taking credit for any dish that met with everyone's approval. "Nonsense, Adrian," Zoé interrupted, "I can't believe you had any part in this gluttony. I know my husband. The deprivations of his childhood make it impossible for him to resist the pleasures of the palate."

"Tell me Zoé," Adrian responded, laughing, "what would you say about your friend here, if I told you that Claire finds it impossible to resist a particular brand of toilet paper whenever it comes on sale? I can hardly open a cupboard door without having rolls of paper hit me in the face."

"Toilet paper is important," Simon offered gravely while they all laughed. "Pride and careers can be brought low by careless attention to such insignificant details. We know something about that, don't we Zoé, my love? Shall I tell them about the time we had the minister of my department and her husband over for dinner?"

Zoé, doubled over with laughter, could only wave her hand in protest while Simon continued. "*Madame le Ministre*, finding nothing appropriate in the guest bathroom for her needs, was forced to call to her husband through the closed door to ask for her handbag where she presumably kept some tissues. She was much too polite to say anything and it was only when I had to avail myself of the same premises that I discovered to my horror how poorly we had entertained her."

"Well, she did hold the portfolio on the status of women at the time," Zoé replied weakly. "I'm sure she was sympathetic to the fact that your wife was so tired from her day's work, she neglected her domestic duties."

"You miss the point, my dear. It was precisely because of her portfolio that she must have blamed me. Why should I, as the Deputy Minister for the Female Condition, expect my wife to attend to such details? No, according to her reasoning, I should have protected you from public embarrassment by taking care of necessary household tasks. By the way," Simon said, turning to Claire and Adrian, "I always check the bathrooms now, so use them without any apprehension."

They were interrupted by the arrival of Juliette, Zoé and Simon's daughter. A tall, grave girl of fifteen, she resembled her father. After embracing her parents and their friends, she sat down on the arm of her father's chair and placed her head on his shoulder, as naturally as if she were still a small child. Zoé and Claire exchanged a private look that acknowledged their conversations about Juliette's attachment to her father. "What's so funny?" the girl asked without raising her head. "I heard you laughing as I came up the stairs."

"Toilet paper," Simon responded, setting off another fit of laughter. Juliette's expression remained unchanged as she continued to watch them in her quiet, solemn fashion.

"Did you have fun with your friends?" Zoé asked her daughter, wiping her eyes.

"It wasn't that kind of an evening, *Maman*," Juliette responded disapprovingly. "I told you, we were meeting for a reason. I suppose you forgot."

"I'm sorry, darling." Zoé said, "I know there's a serious purpose to your meetings, but I thought you might have enjoyed yourself as well." Turning to Adrian and Claire, she explained, "Juliette belongs to a student group against racism. There have been a few nasty incidents at her *lycée* involving Arab children and she and her friends are finding ways to improve the situation. They're very dedicated."

"Do go on," Adrian encouraged the girl. "I'd really like to know more about what you do."

He must be missing his daughter, Claire thought, feeling a slight pang of jealousy. Although Juliette was nothing like Melissa, they shared a similar awkwardness disguised as solemnity. She watched Adrian extend his charm to the young girl, but to no avail.

"I've talked all evening. I need to go to bed," Juliette said, and proceeded to embrace them before retiring. How well brought up French children are, Claire thought, watching the familiar leave-taking ritual.

Their good humor, interrupted by Juliette's glumness, was soon restored. They were not particularly lighthearted people and yet the effect they had on each other was one of buoyancy and playfulness; being together in the same city was reason enough to lift their spirits and fill them with geniality. The good wines Simon continued to offer added to the glow of the evening. Claire heard Adrian invite Simon and Zoé to accompany them the following day to the gardens at Ermenonville outside of Paris. Zoé and Simon, sharing the same good feeling that had prompted Adrian's impulsive offer, accepted at once, forgetting the activities they had planned for that Saturday.

Such an outburst of carefree spontaneity left them momentarily speechless. Recovered from their rashness, they eagerly planned the day's outing with meticulous detail, the very act of planning becoming part of the antici-pated pleasure and thus to be prolonged as long as possible.

After much discussion, they yielded to Simon's warn-ings about weekend traffic and agreed to take the train. But this decision presented new difficulties. The Gare du Nord from which their train departed was deemed too vast and too unfamiliar to Claire and Adrian to serve as a useful meeting place.

"No problem," Adrian said. "We'll pick you up in a taxi and arrive at the station together."

"If only life were that simple," Simon sighed. "In Paris, taxis refuse to carry more than three passengers."

"Perhaps if we arranged for a car in advance, we could find one large enough to take four people," Zoé suggested.

Simon, ever practical, rejected Zoé's plan. "It's hard enough to find any taxi on a Saturday, much less a large one with a driver accommodating enough to run the risk of a fine for harboring a fourth passenger."

"If only we still had our chauffeured car," Zoé said wistfully, regretting the days when Simon's position had entitled them to such privileges.

"Be serious, Zoé. Those days are gone forever." Simon's sharp tone indicated he would prefer not to be reminded of his return to the ranks of anonymous civil servants.

Claire did not contribute to the discussion; she was pleased that no one solicited her views. What a nice change to have others worry about destinations, schedules, meeting places! Their voices became a pleasant background hum as she moved away from the scene, fixing its parameters in her mind as if she had captured it on film. It was an insignificant moment, but it made her feel happy and she wanted to preserve it, to store it like solar energy for darker times.

She became aware of Adrian's hand slowly caressing her back while he continued his conversation with Zoé and Simon and felt a spark of response cut across her dreamy state, pulling her towards him. She suddenly thought of the wild ways they had connected in the past, the endless hours in her flat, in a bed too narrow for the two of them. Now, three years later, her husband's discreet caress contained the memory of that early compelling passion and the reassurance of the steady, quiet love that had replaced it. Marriage was an archive, Claire thought; nothing was lost, if you remembered the code.

Zoé who rarely missed anything, interrupted Simon. "That's enough talking," she said, rising from her chair. "Our friends want to leave and we should all get some sleep if we want to enjoy the day tomorrow."

SIX

Adrian and Claire found Zoé and Simon waiting where they had finally arranged to meet, at the newsstand near the entrance to the train station. Simon, in his usual thoughtful fashion, had already purchased train tickets for all and he now took charge of the party. He led them briskly through the crowded concourse towards the departure platform, stopping to make sure their tickets were stamped by the appropriate machines, explaining to his visitors the intricacies of French train travel as if, Zoé whispered to Claire, they were aborigines emerging from the rain forest. Ignoring Zoé's teasing, he continued to deliver a fact-filled lecture on the merits of the country's high-speed train system, the TGV, which, he informed them, recently set a record for the highest speed of any national rail system: 513 kilometers an hour. "You may not realize that our trains are moving faster than the cruising speed of some aircraft. I think our Japanese friends were properly impressed."

Listening to him, Claire had to agree with Zoé: Simon could be remarkably boring at times. In the presence of foreigners who might fail to recognize his country's civilizing mission in the world, Simon was given to grandiloquent soliloquies. In the beginning Adrian had complained about Simon's lectures — delivered in the same oratorical style whether his audience consisted of a large foreign trade mission or a few friends — but today Adrian showed no sign of annoyance. He and Claire and Zoé followed Simon as happily as schoolchildren on a day's outing.

"Simon and I haven't been out of the city in ages," Zoé said when they settled into their compartment. "You must come more often and shake us out of our dull routines."

"We were away at Christmas," Simon corrected her in his precise way. "Don't you remember, *chérie*? We went to

Milan where I bought these walking shoes," he said, pointing to his feet. "This is the first occasion I've had to try them out. I hope I won't regret the confidence I've placed in the salesman's assurance about their comfort."

Simon's attempt at casual attire on this day — well-pressed flannels, polo shirt, blazer, umbrella and raincoat — was not entirely successful. Zoé, dressed in jeans and a windbreaker, teased him about his appearance. "Simon, you look like a civil servant even when you're on holiday."

Claire worried about Marcel, who was meeting them at their destination. She wished Adrian had listened to her and called Marcel to warn him that they were bringing friends. Marcel was so moody and unpredictable; one never knew how he would react. Adrian told her not to worry, he would handle Marcel. He had considered calling, but decided this would only give Marcel time to fret. Marcel always panicked at the thought of spending time with new people, but Adrian was certain Zoé and Simon were just the sort Marcel would take to once he came to know them.

By the time the train left the suburbs for the open countryside, Claire forgot her uneasiness. The newly green fields, the flowering fruit trees, the neat, well-defined farm enclosures calmed her spirit as the train sped smoothly forward. This farm landscape, she decided, was as pleasing to her as any of the elaborate gardens Adrian admired.

They spotted Marcel as soon as they disembarked from the train. Claire saw at once that her fears had not been groundless. Marcel was visibly shaken by the presence of unexpected guests. A nervous tic, which made him shrug his shoulders and duck his head in semi-circular movements, became more pronounced.

"I don't know how we are going to manage," he said, barely acknowledging Zoé and Simon's presence. "We can't all fit into Sophie's car," he grumbled, pointing in the direction of a small Citröen. A young woman emerged from the car to shake their hands. She was slender, fine-boned, and so fair, her face seemed bleached of all color. Sophie was Marcel's student and she had invited him to spend the weekend at her parents' house, conveniently located near the gardens in Ermenonville.

The little group stood around awkwardly on the empty station platform, uncertain how to proceed while Marcel twitched and muttered in distress. The throes of Marcel's agony had reduced them to silence. Even Simon's skills as a diplomat failed him. There was something so comical about Marcel's petulant contortions and his verbal floundering that Claire avoided Zoé's eyes, fearing a shared look of understanding might send them into helpless laughter.

It was young Sophie who put an end to the uncomfortable scene with surprising grace. "My parents are expecting everyone for lunch before we visit the garden," she said with a smile that included Zoé and Simon. "The house is only two kilometers from the station," she continued. "I'll take three of you now and return for the others." Before leaving, she placed her hand on her teacher's arm, and he responded with a sheepish grin of appreciation.

"I'll walk," Claire decided. To her chagrin, she heard Marcel offer to accompany her. Now that the situation had been taken in hand by Sophie, he appeared to regret his bad temper. "I'm sure Sophie knows what she's doing. She's a remarkable girl."

"You know, Marcel, I did ask Adrian to tell you we were bringing friends," Claire said as they set off on the road to the village. "Let's stop on the way to pick up some extra food for our hosts."

Marcel was breathing heavily at her side from the effort of walking. "Claire, things are not so simple here," he said between gasps. "Your friends seem charming and I'm happy to meet them, but it's an awkward situation. We're in the country here, you see. There are only a couple of food stores in the village and they will probably be closed by the time we reach the village."

At the pace set by Marcel, they would be lucky to get

there by noon, Claire realized. Despite the pleasant, warm day, Marcel wore his usual heavy dark blue sweater and a long scarf wrapped around his neck. Claire had never seen him in any other clothes, and both seemed on the point of unraveling. His labored breathing did not prevent him from talking continuously as they climbed the slight rise in the road.

"Sophie's parents are very special people. You'll like them. The father is the village doctor but every year he goes off to some place like Somalia or Afghanistan to help those who need him. Have you heard of *Médecins sans Frontières*? It's a French organization that sends doctors like Gilbert around the world to troubled areas. Sophie's mother, Anne-Marie, has raised five children. The youngest is eleven. They're all charming. I was in a dreadful state when I arrived at their house yesterday. I had a bad earache and I was running a temperature. The family took wonderful care of me. Gilbert gave me a morphine injection and I had my first good night's sleep in weeks. You understand, I feel indebted to them. This puts me in a difficult position."

Claire began to describe Zoé and Simon Lagarde simply to stop Marcel from agonizing further and to spare his lungs. She found herself embellishing her friends — Simon's illustrious government career, his passion for Stendhal, a fellow civil servant, Zoé's successful practice, their beautiful apartment on rue des Beaux-Arts — knowing that Marcel, for all his hand-to-mouth, garret-style existence, was highly sensitive, like most Europeans, to class distinctions. Marcel, for example, made frequent reference to his illustrious Protestant banking family, although, as he always explained, he belonged to the impoverished, intellectual branch. His only inheritance, he enjoyed telling friends, was a burial vault in the exclusive Montparnasse Cemetery where he is destined to spend eternity in the close company of the poet Charles Baudelaire.

Claire had barely gotten started when she saw Sophie's

car returning to pick them up. She asked Sophie to stop in the village for provisions, but Marcel insisted they first consult Sophie's mother to see what was needed. Sophie, as Claire had expected, obeyed her professor's instructions and Claire found herself catching Marcel's palpable anxiety as she nervously watched the dashboard clock to see if they would make it to the stores before closing.

The next half-hour reminded Claire of a film reel spinning out of control. They arrived at the house. She caught a glimpse of Sophie's father, Gilbert, as he rose from his chair on the terrace to greet them, but before they could shake hands Marcel had propelled her towards the kitchen. Not bothering with introductions, he began to question Sophie's mother, Anne-Marie. Could she use more pâté, more wine more bread? How about some pastries? The local bakery looked promising. What about cheese? Cheese was always good for stretching a meal.

Like her daughter, Anne-Marie smiled calmly throughout Marcel's verbal bombardment. Claire envied their composure; she herself was a captive of Marcel's hysteria. Without waiting for an answer, Marcel had whisked them out of the kitchen, past the terrace, past the blur of puzzled faces, and back into the car. She heard voices calling behind them as they rushed back to the village.

The stores, luckily side by side, were still open. With Marcel hovering over her and nervousness about the passing minutes clouding her judgment, Claire found herself ordering indiscriminately. Sophie tried vainly to restrain her: "I think *maman* made a lemon tart for dessert; I believe there are quiches to start with." But Claire was beyond the power of Sophie's gentle cautionary murmur. The neat, brown paper parcels accumulated on the counter while she kept the clerks busy with more requests. Fortunately, the shopkeepers' respect for the sanctity of the lunch hour was greater than their cupidity and Claire and her companions soon found themselves in the street, with the shutters solidly drawn behind them.

Back at the house, Claire made a point of staying away from Marcel. Who knew what further madness he could induce in her? Marcel, for his part, collapsed into a corner armchair. Claire had seen him often enough to know that his outbursts of excitability were usually followed by periods of exhaustion. She didn't expect him to rally until lunch was served.

The relaxed mood at the table helped Claire to recover her equilibrium. Certainly, there was enough food to satisfy the heartiest appetites. Claire had to admit there probably would have been enough without her purchases. Yet, as platters of *charcuterie*, local cheeses, and garden vegetables began to appear, they added a note of opulence to Anne-Marie's simple meal of leek pie, roast chicken, and lemon tart. The extras from the village stores had turned the meal into a feast, which no one seemed particularly eager to end.

Marcel revived quickly with the food and held forth with his usual verve. When he stopped for a moment to replenish his plate, Anne-Marie turned to Adrian and Claire and asked them if they had been to the theater since they arrived. "There are several interesting new plays this season. The reviews, in any case, have been intriguing, but unfortunately, we haven't managed to see any of them."

"Except for revivals and a few inane comedies, they're all imports," Marcel announced, before Adrian or Claire could respond. "Our cultural landscape is being overrun by an alien force more subtle and dangerous than any we've ever known."

"Marcel is doing his anti-American number," Gilbert explained, turning to Adrian and Claire with an apologetic smile. "He has a low tolerance for any signs of American civilization in our midst."

"Forgive me for contradicting you, Gilbert," Simon volunteered, "but I find civilization a rather grand word to describe the McDonald's and Pizza Huts blighting our cities."

"I don't know," Sophie said. "Sometimes a quick hamburger is much more appealing than a drawn-out meal. But there's so much more to America than fast food. The music, the clothes. My friends and I adore Calvin Klein and the Gap."

"You see what I'm up against?" Marcel growled, striking his forehead in exasperation. "My classrooms are filled with barbarians like Sophie who find it chic to ape American ways. The way they pepper their conversation with English slang, it's a wonder they can still speak their own language."

"I'm sorry to disappoint you Marcel, but I share Sophie's feelings," Zoé responded, giving the girl an encouraging smile. "I've always been a fan of American movies, especially the comedies — the Marx brothers when I was little, and Woody Allen now. The McDonald's may be awful — frankly, I've never been in one — but I become very uneasy when I hear talk of cultural contamination. It smacks of apartheid and ethnic cleansing."

"You may be right," Gilbert agreed, "but the homogenizing effects of economic and cultural globalization are equally disturbing. It's a delicate balance, really, resisting threats to our own culture while avoiding a closed border mentality. You know, every time I visit the US, I'm struck by its diversity and energy. A country forged by immigrants who are proud to call themselves Americans even before they've learned the language. I wish we were half as successful in assimilating our own foreign populations."

"I don't think we need to take lessons from anyone when it comes to the treatment of minorities." Simon's voice had taken on a solemn, pedagogical tone. "France has traditionally been Europe's *terre d'asile*, welcoming political refugees from all corners of the globe. Our credo — Liberty, Equality, Fraternity — has been a symbol of hope wherever oppression thrives. The very notion of left-wing and right-wing politics originated in our National Assembly in 1789. Our ideals are universally admired and our contribution to philosophy, the art of love, food, drink, and fashion are widely imitated. We have every right to see ourselves as a global model of civilization."

"What you say may have been true in the past," Gilbert reluctantly conceded, "but the future, I'm afraid, belongs to the Americans."

"Wasn't that our policy with the Germans under *Maréchal* Pétain? An indecent rush to capitulate and welcome the enemy? What hope is there for our nation if our own citizens lack the will to defend its heritage? Perhaps France as we know it does not deserve to survive." With these words Simon slumped in his chair, making no attempt to hide his desperation.

Claire was shocked to see him looking so wretched. What was going on? Surely, it wasn't only the discussion which left him so visibly shaken. She turned to Zoé for a clue and the worried expression on her friend's face confirmed her unease. Something was not right with Simon.

Simon's pessimism cast a momentary pall over the party. Only Gilbert was still interested in pursuing the argument. "Our mistake is that we spend too much time looking back to our glorious past. Meanwhile, the world around us is changing rapidly and we are in danger of becoming irrelevant. I believe we must take what is best in the New World order and adapt it to our ways. Otherwise, we will end up like the noble Poles who launched a cavalry charge against invading German tanks."

Anne-Marie stood up, pushing her chair back from the table. She seemed angry with her husband for ignoring her attempts to shift the discussion, and Claire was pleased to see that her tranquillity was not boundless. "Gilbert, I need your help in the kitchen," was all she said, however.

When they returned a few minutes later with platters of food, everyone, including Simon, seemed ready to set aside the discussion for the pleasures of the table. As the meal progressed and the wine flowed, the talk became increasingly lighthearted, a free and easy exchange of verbal improvisation and virtuosity that Claire found enchanting. Even Simon forgot his outburst and participated in the playful exchanges. Claire saw the tense little lines around Zoé's mouth relax as she joined in the laughter.

The wordiness of the French was one of the happy discoveries Claire had made during her student year. After the heavy silence of her last years at home, she had welcomed it, although her limited skill with the language relegated her mostly to the role of listener. Now her French was greatly improved, but in the company of such masters she was happy just to admire the performance for as long as it lasted. The words rushing at her from all sides were sparkling spirits of benevolence; as long as they fluttered gracefully around the room, nothing bad could happen to anyone sitting at this table.

The others seemed to share her pleasure in the moment. The good wine, the easy conversation, the open windows with their view of the garden, and the newly green fields made them careless about time. Only Adrian's insistence on visiting Ermenonville finally put an end to the meal.

SEVEN

Claire was glad that Adrian had persuaded them to leave the table. The morning clouds had given way to a sunny April sky. The day had turned warm and she was happy to find herself alone with Adrian while their friends followed at a distance. They were walking down a country road between fields of rape-seed plants budding with yellow flowers and Claire, still under the spell of last night's closeness, wished she and Adrian could lie down in the shelter of all this vegetation. Looking at Adrian, however, she could see that such pleasures were far from his mind at that moment. His excitement was reserved for the gardens they were approaching, whose attractions he was enthusiastically describing to Claire.

Claire had her own reasons for feeling excited about this visit: walking along the road leading to Ermenonville, she knew she was about to retrace Dolly's pilgrimage to the tomb of her mentor. Claire still did not fully understand Rousseau's importance to Dolly. She knew the reasons Dolly gave, her articles of faith — exaltation of nature, mistrust of worldly enticements, an aversion to injustice — but she suspected that for Dolly, as for all of us, great teachers are what we make of them, filling in the spaces between their words with our own version of life, shaping their thoughts to fit our perceptions.

The park had been built in the eighteenth century, Adrian told her, by an idealistic young nobleman, the Marquis René de Girardin. Inspired by Rousseau to renounce society for the benefits of nature, the marquis proceeded to transform a vast, inherited tract of forest, sand dunes, and marshland into a horticultural showplace.

"In his memoirs the marquis wrote, 'Nature and Rousseau were my masters,'" Adrian said, stopping to make a point, "but his writings reveal his own ambition as an artist. He succeeded in using natural elements to create scenes of great beauty and tranquillity. Today the garden is quite shabby and unkempt, but Girardin's hand and Rousseau's influence can still be discerned."

How odd, Claire thought, listening to Adrian. So many years after the marquis, when his garden was nearly overgrown, Dolly had found her own inspiration in the philosopher's teachings. Walking beside Adrian along a leafy path, Claire had a sudden vivid sense of Dolly's presence: a small figure hidden in the loose clothes she favored, striding ahead, eager to capture with a few deft strokes in her sketchbook some aspect of the landscape where once the great man had walked. His spirit, like Dolly's, infused the setting with a sense of enchantment. The lime trees lining the road, the meadows scarlet with wild poppies, the heavy vines nearly obscuring the foot-bridges over streams, were all illuminated by a bright light as if something magical was about to occur. She felt a ripple of anticipation surge through her.

As they resumed walking, Adrian continued his narrative. When the garden neared completion, the marquis offered the beleaguered Rousseau asylum in his newly created Paradise. Hounded by political authorities and his fellow philosophers, a tired and ailing Rousseau accepted Girardin's offer. On the 20th of May, 1778, he made the journey to Ermenonville in the comfortable carriage provided by his new patron. The fantasy world created by the marquis overwhelmed Rousseau and he hoped that here he, along with his faithful companion, Thérèse Le Vasseur, would at last find the peace of mind that had eluded him most of his life. A short while later, he died of a stroke.

"The death of one's idol, while sad in itself, can be highly fortuitous for the admirer: he can now take possession of the legend and enshrine it. Sort of like having Elvis drop dead in your living room," Adrian said, interrupting his account. "Rousseau's death in his newly-created Arcadia provided Girardin with the supreme opportunity to honor his hero, the founder of the nature cult. The shrine he erected was the culmination of Girardin's dream, one he had scarcely dared imagine when he extended his invitation to Rousseau. He immediately ordered a mold to be made of the dead philosopher's face to serve as the basis for future busts of Rousseau. The burial itself, held at midnight beneath a splendid moon, was a highly romantic affair. While villagers lined the banks of the river holding torches, a black boat, illuminated by four candelabras, carried Rousseau's remains silently across the water towards the island ahead of us. What a spectacle!"

Claire could see why Adrian was much sought after as a lecturer. There were times when his eloquence was wasted on her and she simply tuned him out because the subject bored her or because she wanted the conversation to take a different direction. But now she was hanging on to his every word, sharing the excitement his face expressed. "Go on," she urged him; their different preoccupations coincided in this enchanting place.

"Rousseau's tomb became one of the most famous pilgrimage sites in Europe. It was the Graceland of its time, if we're to pursue the Elvis analogy. Napoleon came here, so did the King of Sweden, the Emperor of Austria, Benjamin Franklin, Thomas Jefferson, and other celebrities of the day. Even after his body was moved to the Panthéon in Paris to rest alongside other French notables, the site continued to attract visitors from afar. Apparently, when Napoleon arrived to pay his respects, he was so overcome that he exclaimed, 'I fear time will judge it would have been better if neither he nor I ever existed.' This is but one of the revelations attributed to the magical spirit of this site."

Claire paused to absorb what she had just heard and to allow the others to catch up. Their companions, however, seemed in no hurry to join them. They ambled along, talking and laughing much as they had at the table. Claire felt a little lightheaded, as she had earlier from the wine, but this time it was the site itself and the power of the long-ago events recounted by Adrian that were making her feel pleasantly dreamy. She sensed Adrian's impatience and urged him to walk ahead while she waited for the others. He gave her a grateful look and set off at an energetic stride that quickly took him out of sight.

"What a wonderful day this has turned out to be!" Zoé said, slipping her arm through Claire's. "You know, Claire, you really have a talent for finding people who are gracious and hospitable. In France, as I've always told you, they are rarer than white truffles."

Zoé had first referred to the lack of French hospitality on the day they met when she had taken Claire in and looked after her. Since she rarely traveled, Zoé clung to the belief that the French were amongst the rudest and least gracious people in the world, and continued to warn Claire not to draw any conclusions about her countrymen based on their friendship.

"Gilbert and Anne-Marie are really very nice," Claire agreed, "but what do you make of Marcel?"

"He's amusing, in his own way. But I must say, his tics would drive me crazy if I were to spend much time with him. Did you notice the way he flicks his chin toward his shoulder every now and then? I've never been good at treating people with compulsive twitches. I find myself mimicking them involuntarily. And what's this business with his watch? Why does he keep glancing at it constantly?"

"I can explain that," Claire answered, laughing. "He's madly in love with some woman who is in New York right now. His watch is set on American time so that he can follow her movements throughout the day."

"Let's hope she doesn't return. I suspect he can only handle love at a distance."

Zoé's attention turned to Simon, who was beginning to look warm and uncomfortable in his flannels and wool blazer. "For God's sake, take off your jacket," she said, looking at his flushed face.

Simon ignored her remark and began to talk about Rousseau. He repeated the story she had just heard about Napoleon's visit to the philosopher's tomb. Simon's version was more elaborate and took twice as long to tell. When he finished, Zoé laughingly reported to Claire, "Simon read late into the night after you left, so that he could impress you with such historical gems."

Claire liked Simon too well to encourage Zoé's teasing. Lately, Zoé's tone with Simon had become excessively mocking, she felt, and it made her uncomfortable. Simon could be long-winded at times, and his genteel manners occasionally bordered on the ridiculous, but she rather enjoyed his gallantry, and unlike Zoé, who must have heard it all too often, she listened gratefully to his discourses on French history. "How old was Rousseau when he came here?" she asked Simon.

"Oh, if you're going to encourage him . . ." Zoé said, and ran ahead.

"Be careful, darling," Simon shouted after her. "Zoé broke her ankle this winter playing tennis and it's still a bit wobbly," he explained to Claire. "Now, about Rousseau. He was sixty-six years old when he finally accepted the invitation of the Marquis de Girardin, which is really like being in one's eighties today. An old man in poor health and severely depressed, according to the letters he wrote to friends. He was embroiled in a variety of feuds with the authorities who had condemned his works, he had alienated most of his friends and patrons with endless demands and accusations of betrayal, and he was plagued by constant worries about money. The marquis' invitation was a godsend. When he saw the gardens for the first time he was deliriously happy. Here he found reassurance that his ideas were valued and applied with fervor. He embraced the marquis and said, 'My heart has been longing to come here for a long time and now my eyes convince me that I desire to remain here forever.' Had he lived, he would have probably fallen out with his latest patron as well, but as it was, death spared him that final deception. Watch out, Claire, it's a bit muddy up ahead."

"What a memory you have, Simon."

"Actually, Zoé's right, I did do a bit of homework before coming here." He took her arm and gently steered her past the pools of water dotting their path. "Ah, here we are. The first important site. Rousseau's tomb. Did you know that in Rousseau's time it was considered obligatory to weep when you reached this point in the pilgrimage? Let's rest for a minute on that bench and contemplate it as all visitors in the past have done. Wearing these new Italian shoes today may have been a mistake, I think." Simon sighed with relief when they were seated. "As I said, the tomb's power to stimulate the imagination is said to be legendary. Like Lourdes."

Their stone bench faced a lake. Across the water, they could see a small island surrounded by poplars. Rousseau's tomb, a Roman-style sarcophagus, was visible between the colonnade of trees. Claire had to agree with the descriptions she had heard. It was an evocative scene. The island, the leaning poplars, the simple stone sarcophagus seemed to float in an aura of calm and melancholy.

Simon articulated her thoughts. "It's easy to feel the hand of history here, isn't it?" he said. "Can't you see Rousseau walking these paths, finding consolation in the tranquillity of these scenes? I think that's what I need," he added after a pause. "A long period of solitude, preferably in the country. I don't seem to do well in company these days."

"Don't be silly," Claire said, patting his arm. "You're marvelous with people." She knew he regretted his earlier outburst, but her reassurance failed to convince him. "Thank you, Claire, but I'm afraid I'm really no good to anyone right now."

They sat quietly for a while, Simon's dejection adding to the melancholy of the scene. She was trying to think how she might cheer him up, when Adrian found them. He looked especially happy today, she noticed, grateful for his easy disposition. She embraced him as if they were meeting after a long separation. Adrian, taken aback, responded in a distracted fashion. Disentangling himself from her arms, he said, "I came back to tell you about the inscription carved on the tomb. I was afraid you might miss it. It reads, 'Here lies a man of nature and of truth.'"

Simon, quick to hide his distress from Adrian, jumped to his feet, ready for debate. "What irony. A man dedicated to the truth, who couldn't stop lying," he began, his voice tinged with scorn. "That's the key to Rousseau's tragedy. The liar who loved truth. Look at the way he tried to justify the fact that he had consigned all five of his children to a foundling hospital, like unwanted kittens to be disposed of at will. This from a man who concerned himself with the welfare of children and wrote books advocating a new approach to education and respect for children's rights. He even defended the rights of infants to be with their mothers by speaking out against the custom then prevalent among fashionable women of handing their children over to wet nurses. He started a debate about breast-feeding that still continues. What a hypocrite!"

Adrian rose to the bait as Claire knew he would, but she was not interested in their argument. Two cocks, snapping at each other's feathers, she thought unkindly, happy to see them walk away. Their words interfered with her own emerging sense of the man — not the great philosopher her mother had held up for admiration, but the flesh and blood person, frail and exhausted by life, seeking comfort in nature. After years of ignoring Rousseau simply because he had belonged to Dolly, she felt the power of the old man's presence here where he had lived and died. She wanted to be alone with him, as Dolly had been, in this place where the passage of time was so easily forgotten.

Adrian and Simon were well out of sight, but Claire lingered, reluctant to move. There was something about the unchanging nature of this place — the stillness of the lake, the floating white marble sarcophagus, the infinite patience of the poplars leaning into the wind — that affected her deeply.

The wind picked up, rustling the newly green leaves, whispering its mournful dirge. It seemed to be speaking straight to her heart. She closed her eyes. The word "fools," whispered yet distinct, came from somewhere nearby. She looked around and saw no one. She concentrated on the sound, attuning her mind to the wind. Now it resembled the voice of an old man laughing in derision. Claire almost joined in. For weeks, she had been reaching out to Dolly and instead she had conjured up the voice of a strange old man.

Years ago, soon after Dolly's death, Claire had a disturbing dream in which Dolly turned into the family cat. When Claire tried to caress her, the cat vanished beneath the garden fence. In dreams that followed, Claire found herself looking vainly, often desperately, for the elusive cat, only to wake up in a state of great agitation to find the real cat safely asleep at the foot of her bed. Had Dolly again assumed some form other than her own — Rousseau's, for example? Listening to the whispers mocking Adrian and Simon's conversation some distance away, she decided the voice she heard had to be Rousseau's. "Fools," she heard quite clearly this time, "learned fools. You're wise not to follow their vain parroting."

Claire felt she ought to defend Adrian and Simon, but she was not about to enter into a discussion with a disembodied voice. The voice did not alarm her unduly. She had always been easy prey for lost souls. In airports, at parties, people attached themselves to her just in this way — a voice reaching out to her, unknown, unwanted, interrupting her thoughts —as if her pursuers saw in her face some sign inviting them to approach. And they were right. Invariably, she gave them her attention, at least for a while. She did the same with the new intruder, a voice that came at once from within her and from this place, its message carried in the shifting sounds of the wind, the swaying of the treetops and the responding beat of her own heart.

EIGHT

Claire rose tentatively from the bench. She was not displeased to find the voice following. "What a sad state has befallen these gardens. When I first came here I thought I had found Paradise, but it proved to be a short-lived illusion. I was brought here, I soon learned, for the marquis' amusement, to be trotted out and made to perform whenever he felt so inclined. I yearned for my bed while he commanded brilliance. It's difficult for the mind to shine when your body aches with weariness and your bowels remain locked in a stubborn vise, squeezing the life out of you . . ."

"Claire, wait up," Zoé called. "I see you've given Simon the slip," she said when she caught up with Claire. "Had enough of his erudition?"

Claire ignored Zoé's teasing. "Tell me," she asked instead, "do you have patients who hear voices?"

"What an odd question. Adolescents in general have very febrile imaginations. They hear all kinds of voices except those of their parents or teachers, who seem to have difficulty reaching them. I have a sixteen-year-old patient, very intelligent, very imaginative, who is visited regularly by a formless creature from outer space who gives him hints on how to dress and how to wear his hair. He looks so bizarre, Claire, that if you saw him, you would believe he is the object of alien inspiration. In a clear-cut case of schizophrenia, drugs do wonders. Why do you ask?"

"Well, I don't know how to say this, but I have just been listening to a voice and I think it belongs to Rousseau. Don't laugh. I heard him as clearly as I hear you now."

"How wonderful. I envy you, I really do. You must have spiritual gifts I never suspected. I am afraid I'm much too ordinary and dull to merit such a windfall."

"Come off it, Zoé. Next thing I know, you'll be telling me to set up shop as a medium, or a channeler."

"Well, why should kooks have a monopoly on spiritualism?"

"I'm not finding this amusing. I really think my episode, for want of a better word, falls into your domain. Why me? Why did he pick me?"

"Why not?" Zoé responded, still laughing. "Maybe it's like those apparitions of the Virgin Mary. Did you notice she always appears to simple souls, not to say the simple-minded? I mean, have you ever heard of a sighting by anyone with any claim to intellectual rigor? The same thing is true of the people who are contacted by aliens from outer space. You've got to admit, you're more intuitive than intellectual. You've told me often enough how difficult you find some of Adrian's abstract arguments."

"Thanks a lot for that flattering assessment. I see you're not going to take me seriously." She'd had enough of Zoé's teasing. The strange visitation had shaken her more than she'd realized.

Zoé put her arm around her. "Really Claire, we've known each other for years. I'm not going to start worrying about your mental stability now. Do you want me to say you're hallucinating? Would it make you feel better? Or that your subconscious is playing games with you? After all, you've told me often enough how your mother plied you with daily doses of Rousseau along with cod liver oil. Whether you wanted to or not, you must have internalized her words. Now, for reasons of its own, your mind brings that voice forward. But I really don't want to analyze it. Nor should you. I'm sure it's a passing thing, so enjoy it while it lasts."

Claire felt reassured. Zoé had a wonderful way of making the bizarre seem normal. She couldn't really blame Zoé for her teasing. She remembered her own reaction when Lucinda had told her about a vision she'd had during a tree-hugging exercise at her ashram. Claire's gentle ridicule had left them crying from laughter. Fortunately,

Lucinda never lost her sense of humor, whatever guise she assumed. Now it was Claire's turn to be mocked and she accepted it good-naturedly. Yet she knew what she had heard and doubted the voice had had its final say.

"By the way," Zoé asked, resuming a lighthearted tone, "what was he whispering in your ear? Or is it too private to share?"

"Well, if you must know, he was complaining. Apparently, he suffered from chronic constipation, arthritis, and a need to urinate with astonishing frequency."

"It must be his Swiss childhood. No, really, constipation is a national disease in Switzerland. I've just read a paper on the subject in one of my professional journals. The author quoted Cocteau, who wrote something wonderful about the erotic sensation Rousseau experienced at the age of ten when a woman teacher spanked him on his bare bottom. It went something like this: "The blushing behind of Jean-Jacques is the rising sun of Freud.' Meaning that Rousseau's writings anticipated the psychoanalytic process. That, I'm afraid, is the extent of my Rousseau lore. Aren't you relieved? What a glorious day! I'm tempted just to stretch out under a tree and forget the sightseeing. Want to join me?"

Claire laughed and confessed her little fantasy of making love among the flowering rape-seed plants.

"How marvelous," Zoé sighed. "Even when Simon and I were first together, I could never have imagined him doing anything so rash."

They ambled on across a series of footbridges towards an expansive view of ancient trees bending over streams, framing glimpses of grottos, waterfalls, and the remains of follies. When the path they had been following turned, they saw Marcel resting on a rock. "Please don't say anything about our conversation," Claire whispered to Zoé.

"Of course, darling," Zoé promised. "Your visitation will be our secret, but only if you keep me as your confidant."

Marcel rose to greet them. "Two laughing wood nymphs coming to my rescue. I don't think I would have had the energy to continue on my own. No one seems to have noticed my absence. I suppose they just surged ahead without giving me a second thought. May I lean on you to make the ascent?"

Claire and Zoé looked startled at the prospect of propelling Marcel's bulk up the slope.

"No, no," he said seeing their expressions. "I didn't mean it literally. All I require is your pleasant company. Give me a minute to catch my breath."

"I think if you removed your muffler, you might find it a little easier to breathe," Zoé suggested. "The day has turned warm, you know."

"How kind of you to be concerned, my beautiful Zoé, but you see I'm an asthmatic."

"I'm afraid I don't follow."

"I know what my poor body needs. The muffler is essential."

"As a security blanket," Zoé whispered to Claire, and they both giggled.

"Wood nymphs always laugh at the awkwardness of mortals. But tell me: what secrets made you laugh before I became the focus of your sly amusement? I saw you being quite merry as you came up the road."

"We were speculating about Rousseau's romantic life," Claire said, not averse to teasing Marcel with Zoé at her side.

"What an apt topic on such a fine day. Did you know that his extreme timidity as a young man made him impotent? I don't mean in the vulgar sense. Physiologically his member responded with reflexive predictability, but in the presence of women he adored, he became instantly terrified. How well I understand him. Like me, he preferred the company of two women to being alone with one. It was easier for him to converse when the prospect of physical eroticism was impeded by the presence of the beloved's friend."

"Really? No *ménage à trois* ?"

"My poor Zoé, you are a decadent child of your time. Rousseau was a simple boy raised by austere Swiss Puritans. I too am the descendant of Swiss Protestants and I know what I'm talking about. For Jean-Jacques, women were objects of romance and exaltation, not receptacles of lust. He used his peasant hand for that. Sexual perversity was really quite beyond him. It required the talents of an older woman to teach him about voluptuousness and turn him into a libertine. Unfortunately, I have never had the good fortune to fall into the hands of such willing teachers, so I'm afraid I'm still stuck at that early phase of Rousseau's erotic development where women must make all the advances." He looked at them in a most appealing fashion as he said this, and Zoé and Claire burst out laughing.

"You may laugh, but it's really quite tragic, I assure you. The sexual revolution has passed me by entirely. Now, with the advent of AIDS, it's too late. Fortunately, celibacy becomes more attractive with age."

"I don't think I want to touch that," Zoé said, but the women slowed their pace to accommodate Marcel. The effort of the climb left him too breathless to speak. The three of them slowly made their way up the hill.

They reached the top and found the others gathered around the ruins of a Doric temple, listening to Adrian. He waved a hand in their direction and waited for them to draw near before resuming his narrative. "The temple was deliberately left unfinished," Adrian continued, "to express the idea that philosophy never attains the pure understanding it strives for. The composition is a fine example of Romantic eclecticism . . ."

Claire could not concentrate on Adrian's words. The old man had spoiled it for her. She felt him hovering nearby, mocking Adrian's learned exposition. "He's a fool to ignore you," he whispered on cue. A shiver of excitement swept through her and instinctively she stepped back from the group. The voice grew louder. "The experience of the senses, the quickening of the heart, the feel of warm flesh — these are worth all the temples in the world."

Claire heard the old man sigh so deeply she could almost feel his breath on her skin. She felt herself growing bolder. If the voice originated within her, as Zoé said, then why not steer it where she wished? She thought of Rousseau's erotic history as Marcel had just described it — this information had not been part of Dolly's instructions — and sure enough, the voice resumed. "Women have been the true joy of my life. Whatever wisdom I possessed, proceeded from nature and from women who, through their touch, their warmth, their generosity, taught me everything I know. They were far more persuasive teachers than any schoolroom tyrant."

The old man seemed to pay silent homage for a moment to his long-ago lovers. "Once, en route between Chambery and Montpellier," he resumed in a voice thickened by emotion, "I found myself in a carriage with a rather plain, heavy-set woman, long past her youth, whom I chose to ignore, preferring the book I held in my hand. I am ashamed to say I was innocent of any curiosity about my traveling companion, and did not bother to exchange the usual polite phrases required on such occasions. The good lady had to make all the advances, using the experience of her fifty-odd years to capture my attention. Finally she succeeded and I put down my book. Had I not trusted the touch of her hand on mine, I would have gone to my death without knowing the most exquisite sensual delights concealed by my companion's unprepossessing appearance. The ecstasy we shared in that brief encounter continued to warm my heart until my dying day."

Claire had come across this story in her reading, but hearing it now, told in a voice as weary as the world, filled her with strange sensations. Although she worked with images, she had always found words, the right words, far more erotically stimulating. She suddenly thought of a lover she'd once had, a man she had not particularly liked, yet his verbal inventiveness during their lovemaking had been so exciting, the affair continued despite her repeated resolutions to end it. Perhaps Rousseau was the kind of lover married women invented when they wanted to remain married.

"Are you all right?" She felt a hand on her arm and turned to find Simon beside her. The others had moved on. "Shall we continue?" he asked, taking her arm. "You seemed so lost in thought, I didn't dare disturb you. In any case, I needed the rest. Let's try to catch up with the others or they might start to worry."

His dark mood seemed to have lightened for the moment, Claire noticed, and she hoped it would not return now that they were alone. "I doubt Adrian would notice my absence," she said, offering one of her own semi-serious concerns to keep him distracted. "He's far more interested in inanimate objects these days."

"What's this? Feeling neglected?" Simon responded with enthusiasm. "My dear Claire, that's part of marriage. It's one of the conditions I like best about the marital state. It's such a relief to be able to take someone for granted and to know that person feels the same way about you. There are evenings when Zoé is working on her crossword puzzle while I describe something that happened at the ministry, and I know she scarcely hears a word I'm saying. It fills me with great tenderness to see her absorption, her absent-mindedness. It means she is as relaxed with me as if she were alone. I know she's obliged to listen carefully all day to her patients and I'm aware she's heard my complaints hundreds of times. So there we are, ensconced in our evening routine, comforted by its familiarity. It's like finding your way to the bathroom at night in the dark, and knowing exactly where every obstacle lies: the door, the sofa, the stand with the vase on it, that lamp that leans at an odd angle — there is no need to turn on a light to see your way. Marriage is like that, a familiar terrain where you can navigate with lights dimmed."

Claire laughed, happy to enjoy Simon's wit again. "I'm very serious Claire," Simon continued with mock gravity. "Once you've accepted the state of affectionate lethargy that settles over most good marriages, it can be deeply comforting. You no longer have to worry about the sentimental side of life — that part is settled — and you are free to concentrate on other ambitions. Adrian, I suspect, is thinking of his new book. I would even go so far as to say that Adrian's ability to ignore you while he worries about his new book — let's not forget he has the specter of his previous success to contend with as he writes — comes from the sureness of his feelings for you."

Simon was no doubt right about Adrian. She would do better to listen to him than to a strange voice. It was no use building a case against Adrian when it was her own unmoored state which made her see things in a skewed way. To change the subject, she said, "What a charming cabin," pointing to a structure ahead of them.

The lush greenery had given way to a landscape of sand, rock, and clusters of scotch pines. A path on their right climbed steeply to the top of a hill where a simple thatched stone house rose from the side of a rock outcrop. Adrian and the others were waiting at the foot of the hill. He was engrossed in photographing the stone cabin while Marcel, off to one side, appeared to be photographing Adrian. For the first time that day, Claire took out her camera and focused it on Marcel photographing Adrian who was photographing the cabin. This was the love affair of the day, she could not help thinking as she clicked away, despite her resolve not to give way to childish petulance.

When she lifted her head, she saw their host, Gilbert, running up the mountain as swiftly and effortlessly as a mountain goat.

"It must be all those trips to Afghanistan," Simon murmured beside her. Gilbert waved when he reached the top and incongruously lit a cigarette. Claire was not surprised to see Zoé, who responded to physical challenges with instinctive rivalry, follow Gilbert at a pace equal to his.

Unlike his wife, Simon, with his fair skin and rotund shape, was not at his best in outdoor activities. "Well, my children," he said to the rest of the group, "I think I will wait for you here."

"I'll stay with you," Claire offered.

"No, no," Simon protested, "you must climb up. The cabin you see is the house the marquis built for Rousseau — *la cabane du philosophe.* It's been a place of pilgrimage since the eighteenth century. Who knows when you'll be back here again?"

Claire was the last one to reach the top. She thought the high-perched, primitive dwelling was more suitable for an adventurous young man than an aging philosopher. She was not surprised to hear Marcel say that Rousseau had never actually lived in the house. "Rousseau was supposed to reside here as a sort of ornamental hermit. Every fashionable nobleman aspired to have one on his estate. The philosopher, however, preferred a comfortable cottage near the castle. On the second of July, 1778, the steep climb proved fatal. He died a few hours later, stricken by a cerebral hemorrhage. Even superior beings, like the rest of us, die an ordinary death."

"I don't know what you mean by an ordinary death," Gilbert said without looking at anyone in particular. "Since I became a physician I've seen thousands of deaths. There is nothing ordinary about any of them. It's not a spectacle one ever takes for granted."

Marcel, chastised by the doctor's words, sank to the ground near Claire. "An extraordinary man," he whispered in Claire's ear. "I have great admiration for him." Claire was not clear whether he meant Rousseau or Gilbert.

She found Adrian at her side. The fresh air and the sight-seeing had heightened his color, making him look very handsome, she thought. "I've missed you," he whispered in her ear. "Where have you been?"

This was not the moment to tell him about the voice, Claire decided. "I've been here. Following like a faithful dog." She saw him frown and regretted her words.

"Really, Claire. What's gotten into you? I see you flitting in and out of the group, but even when you're with us you're somewhere else."

"Strange. I feel the same way about you."

He stared at her, puzzled. "Am I boring you again, is that it?"

She wanted to tease his frown away. "What does it matter? Everyone else is hanging on to your every word. And there's always Marcel."

She hadn't succeeded. "I suppose this is your way of punishing me for neglecting you," he said.

"Have you been neglecting me?" Even as she continued the game — and it was merely a game, there was no rancor in her heart — she reminded herself that she had been drawn to Adrian because of his devotion to his work. A serious man like Adrian, she had thought, would never allow his life to be wasted by insignificant distractions. She had learned Dolly's credo well and still believed it.

"I can see how you might feel ignored. I'll make it up to you, I promise."

Claire thought again of the field filled with yellow flowers, but the moment had passed. "I'm fine, really," she said putting her arm through his. "I *am* a little jealous of Marcel, however," she added playfully. "He's had his eye on you all day. And who can blame him?"

"You are a wicked, wicked woman," he said, but she saw that he was relaxed again. Pleased with herself, she squeezed his hand hard.

"Wicked and strong. The woman I always dreamt about."

NINE

They left the park in two groups. Zoé, Simon, and Marcel drove off in Sophie's car, while Claire and Adrian accompanied Gilbert and Anne-Marie. They would all meet at the house before taking the train back to Paris.

Instead of heading home directly, Gilbert took them on a quick tour of the countryside, which ended abruptly at the gates of a large stone house. "You know, as a country doctor, I take care of everyone in the area," he said turning around to face his passengers. "The count who owns this château lives in Paris. But his mother still resides here with a servant couple. I think it would be interesting for you to meet her and see the place. The grounds are said to be the work of André Le Nôtre, the greatest of French gardeners, who designed the gardens at Versailles, as you are no doubt aware."

"What about the others? They'll be waiting for us," his wife, Anne-Marie, interjected in her soft voice. But Gilbert was already out of the car, running up the circular driveway to the house. Anne-Marie's calm exterior, Claire was beginning to suspect, was a sort of armor to protect her from Gilbert's rapid-fire impulses which propelled him as easily across the world as across the road.

He reappeared a few minutes later, waving for them to follow. They soon found themselves in a small dim room, lined with ornately framed portraits, in the presence of the old countess.

Even in the semi-darkness of the room, her appearance was so startling that Claire had to will herself not to stare. A tiny woman, well into her eighties, the countess wore the make-up of a clown: turquoise lines shadowed her lids, circled her eyes, outlined her brows, and the color was repeated in a matching ribbon pinned to her bright red hair;

85

small red circles dotted her cheeks while a slash of crimson, haphazardly applied, approximated the outline of her lips. From the neck down, she was dressed entirely in black, which set off dramatically the vivid colors of her face. "How nice of you to come," she said, greeting them as if they were expected guests. "Life in the country can be very monotonous."

Claire instantly wanted to photograph her, in this very room with its faded baroque opulence admirably framing her extravagant appearance, but it was too soon to ask. She hoped an opportunity would come later.

While Gilbert and Anne-Marie chatted with the countess about local matters, Adrian and Claire were encouraged to view the adjoining reception rooms. "It's a typical old country château, no longer at its best, I'm afraid, but a novelty for you perhaps." They dutifully examined a succession of large and small rooms filled with dark paintings, faded tapestries, hunting rifles, ornate vases, and heavy bronze statues mostly of dogs and horses. Claire wondered if the countess' extraordinary appearance was an attempt to distinguish herself from the lackluster décor of these rooms. Certainly the intimate salon, as the countess called her sitting room, was far more whimsical than what they saw of the rest of the house.

"Come over here, my dear, and let me have a better look at you," Claire heard the countess call to her in a surprisingly strong voice. "I understand you are a photographer," she said, inviting Claire to take the chair near her. "I myself was something of an amateur photographer in my younger days. In my time, young ladies were allowed to be only amateurs. Papa, who enjoyed the company of artists, once brought home Monsieur Jacques-Henri Lartigue, you may have heard of him. He was kind enough to compliment me on my little scenes. Now my hands shake so badly, I can no longer hold a camera steady." She held up her trembling hands for evidence. Claire noticed the color of her nails that matched the vibrant scarlet of her mouth and the rings adorning every finger.

"They're copies," she said following Claire's gaze. "The real ones were sold long ago. This house requires a sacrifice every year. Something always needs to be repaired. And I need *my* adornments, even if they're fake. When beauty goes, eccentricity becomes a suitable substitute." She placed her hands in her lap, smoothing the fabric of her dress, which, Claire noticed, could have done with a good brushing. "I would be very interested in your opinion of my photographs. My favorite subjects were the grounds of the château. I suppose the good doctor has already told you they were designed by Le Nôtre. Being a proper *gauchiste* does not prevent a man from being a snob."

"I would like that very much. Unfortunately, we're returning to Paris tonight."

"Why don't you come again, on your own? I'm alone most of the time. My son and his family are here only the odd weekend. I'm not the sort of person who minds solitude, but an occasional visit does break the monotony. Thomas, my chauffeur, will meet you at the train. We can have tea *à deux* and look through the family albums."

"It sounds lovely."

"Good. Here is my card. You will let me know which train you're taking. No *Monsieur*, I'm afraid you're not included in this invitation," she said to Adrian, who had come over to join them, "but you are welcome any other time. I'm told you're interested in gardens. Would you like to see the grounds before you leave? I can give you a quick tour of all the choice spots. Guaranteed four-star views."

Adrian mentioned they had friends waiting and a train to catch, but the countess insisted. She would have them back at the house in no time. "I thought you Americans like to do things on the run," she said, leading the way out. She instructed Adrian to sit beside her while Claire, Gilbert and Anne-Marie climbed into the back seat.

Propped up on a tapestry cushion to help her see over the steering wheel, the countess, true to her word, drove across her property with a speed that rivaled Gilbert's. Every now and then she brought the car to a sudden stop at some particularly picturesque spot — an unexpected long perspective in the midst of the woods that suddenly revealed the château from a new angle; an architectural ornament in a hidden clearing; a stream flowing between clumps of wild irises — and waited for Adrian to photograph it.

"There's no need to get out of the car," she reassured him. "I've positioned the vehicle so that all you have to do is point your camera." The countess' manner had become quite bossy, but Adrian obeyed with good grace. Claire could not imagine anyone not obeying the countess, for all her slight stature.

The countess kept her promise and returned them to the château in less than an hour. Before they left, she took Claire aside and repeated her invitation with some insistence. Claire found the attention flattering but wondered why it was being directed at her. She promised to return soon.

"What was that all about?" Gilbert asked when they were in the car driving back to his house.

"The countess has invited me to visit. It's a tempting offer. I would love to photograph her."

"You should," Gilbert said from the front seat. "She is a fascinating woman who has led a very interesting life. She represents a slice of French society — *la vieille France* — that is fast disappearing. You're lucky she took to you."

"Everyone takes to Claire," Adrian said, putting his arm around her. "And no one can resist her camera. I speak from experience."

"Did you find her garden interesting?" Gilbert asked Adrian. He had no doubt heard about Adrian's research from Marcel.

"It's lovely, but it's outside the scope of my book. I'm concentrating on the great formal gardens that are still maintained in their original state. Here, I'm afraid, Le Nôtre's plan is barely discernible." Claire was pleased to hear Adrian's response. If she returned, as the countess had urged her to do, she wanted the place to herself.

Zoé, Simon, Marcel, and Sophie were waiting at the house. Marcel was most annoyed when he learned of their meeting with the countess. They had missed the train, he pointed out with irritation, and would have to wait two hours for the next one. The appearance of coffee and a platter of the sweets Claire had purchased with such haste earlier in the day helped to restore his spirits. The names of the cakes — *religieuse, vacherin, madeleine, mille-feuilles* — prompted him to deliver a lecture on their origin, as they disappeared one by one into his mouth.

It had been a long, full day and Marcel had the platter and the floor to himself. Noting the quiet mood of his companions, he reached into his shabby, bulging briefcase and produced a well-worn copy of Rousseau's *Reveries*. "I think you will find the philosopher's words a fitting way to end the day," he said, and began to read: "Of all the places where I have lived (and I have known some charming ones) none has made me so truly happy nor left me with such tender regrets as the island of St. Pierre, in the middle of the lake of Bienne."

Marcel's friends listened, enchanted, as his deep voice caressed Rousseau's prose, still vibrant so long after his death. The lush description of the island and Rousseau's evocation of his idyllic life there were as comforting as a fairy tale — a fairy tale for the times. Outside, nature was under assault as never before, but Rousseau's words offered the soothing promise of a paradisiacal landscape in perpetual equilibrium.

The odd little countess in her vast and deserted château belonged to the fairy tale as well, Claire thought. What a strange and wonderful day it had been! And to think she had Marcel to thank for it. The idea that she was feeling gratitude towards Marcel, the same Marcel who had nearly ruined everything this morning with his temper tantrum, was so startling, it caused her to smile. Surely this was the strangest of the day's many surprises.

TEN

Claire and Adrian were now living with Marta.

Adrian had been reluctant to give up the small studio Marcel had found for them near the Bibliothèque Forney where he spent his days doing research for his book. Claire had stressed the money they would save and the extra space they would enjoy in Marta's large flat. She held out the promise of Marta's tranquil street, a relief from the endless rush of traffic and the subterranean clatter of the Metro they were forced to endure in their studio. She did not mention, however, the confidences she hoped to elicit from Marta about Dolly's past once they were living under the same roof. For the time being, she preferred to keep her investigation to herself.

Claire suspected Adrian would not encourage her attempts to probe into her mother's life. His work as an art historian entitled him to rifle through all manner of evidence, including the most private documents, for the sake of scholarship, but in personal matters Adrian could be maddeningly secretive. All of Claire's teasing curiosity about her predecessor, the very public Pamela Porter, had produced few satisfying details about their life together. Claire would have particularly enjoyed hearing about the deficiencies concealed by Pamela's external perfection, but her probing made Adrian visibly uncomfortable and she was forced to abandon it. Unlike some of her previous lovers, Adrian appeared to have no need to blame his ex-wife, a quality Claire finally had to admire.

Adrian's reticence made her consider the propriety of her undertaking. What right did children have to their parents' secrets? Were the letters of a family member any more taboo than those of the mistress of a celebrated painter? Considerations of this sort were subject to the moral climate of the day. Society now sanctioned the right of adopted children to seek out their natural parents. Whatever the general wisdom might be, Claire was convinced of the validity of her search: wresting secrets from the dead was a kind of triumph against the indifference of time. When she died, who would care about Dolly's secrets?

The urgency she felt was not the product of mere curiosity. Her mother's disintegration, which she had painfully witnessed as a child, had been vividly revived by her own crisis — those desperate flights, running for her life like a hunted creature, running from work she had once loved. She didn't know whether a link really existed, a causal link, between her own troubles and her mother's. She was convinced, however, that in understanding Dolly's decline, she would find clues to her own shaky state. This conviction was like a talisman; she invested it with her belief and it brought her comfort. She could not let go of it.

Marta's apartment, on a narrow, medieval street close to the Place de la République, was large enough to accommodate Claire and Adrian with room to spare. In the years she had lived there, Marta had managed to crowd the rooms with stacks of books, newspapers, magazines, the documents she translated, folders filled with correspondence, unwanted gifts, and all sorts of debris that entered her household, never to leave it. The departure of her daughter, Louise, and the death of her beloved Bruno had allowed her to extend her activities and belongings to the vacant rooms. Now space had to be cleared for Claire and Adrian. Claire and Marta worked side by side emptying the two rooms she and Adrian were to occupy. Adrian had offered to help but was dissuaded by Claire, who wanted Marta all to herself.

If Marta minded the upheaval created by her guests she gave no sign of it. If anything, she upbraided herself for not being more attentive to them. When Claire and Adrian protested that, really, they preferred to come and go as they pleased and not be bound by set hours for meals, Marta admitted that she herself liked to be treated with a minimum of fuss whenever she stayed with friends. Nevertheless, she insisted that as soon as she had a free minute, she would make a proper dinner and bring them together with her daughter and her family.

"Don't count on it," Claire told Adrian, watching the flurry of activities and concerns that filled Marta's days. Preparations for her hearings with the tax people required endless meetings with elusive bureaucrats, and left her burdened with forms needing to be stamped by other unhelpful officials. The precarious health of her numerous friends meant that Marta always had someone to visit, to cheer up, to sooth. Her friend Gertrude was becoming increasingly despondent about her husband's condition and telephoned daily for comfort.

Marta's greatest worry was for her grandson, Antoine, whose shiftless existence so exasperated her daughter and son-in-law that they threatened to put him out. She talked constantly about Antoine to Claire and to Adrian, trying to find some way to motivate the young man. "I have to believe in him," she explained, "no one else does. If only I could find a way to help him connect to something outside himself." Antoine displayed a vague interest in the arts, Marta said, and offered as evidence the fact that he had managed to track down an obscure publication featuring an article on Adrian's work. She urged Adrian to talk to him. Adrian promised he would.

Henri, who came by regularly, found a new reason for urging Marta to move in with him. Why not leave her flat to her guests, he suggested reasonably, and dispense with all the fuss of clearing space for them to occupy.

"But I want to be around to help them," Marta protested feebly. "What sort of hostess would I be abandoning them to themselves?"

When Henri left, Marta told Claire how much she disliked his apartment. Henri's *quartier*, in the tenth *arrondissement*, was too quiet, too lifeless at night, and his rooms so crammed with furniture that Marta found it stifling to be there for any length of time. Henri was willing to move anywhere Marta chose, although he admitted a preference for a modern house on the outskirts of Paris. She confessed a horror of becoming "a little old lady tending her garden in the suburbs."

Claire understood that Marta was as unlikely to move in with Henri as she was to produce the promised family dinner. "We don't just disagree on where to live," Marta elaborated, "we disagree on everything. His political views make me cringe. When Henri was young, he was part of our progressive circle. I used to see him and his wife, who was a dear friend of mine, at all the marches and meetings Bruno and I attended. But now he's wrapped himself in conservatism and there's no use talking to him. I try to avoid discussing politics with Henri. Yet, I can't help feeling guilty whenever I think of Bruno. I suppose it says something about my marriage to Bruno that I feel guilty about Henri's politics, but not about the presence of another man in my life."

Marta kept her confidences for Claire and made sure Adrian's work went undisturbed. She had cleared Bruno's study and when Adrian was not at the library he spread out his papers and books on Bruno's old mahogany desk. "It's nice to see the room used again," Marta said, and Claire agreed. Although the two men had never met, it pleased her to know that Adrian worked where Bruno had spent his days, protected from the world by Marta. Now Marta extended that protection to Adrian.

Adrian was pleased with the move. It was a relief, he told Claire, not to have to pack up everything at night as he had been obliged to do in the studio where he had worked on the dining room table. And she had been right about the quiet of Marta's street; he was sleeping much better since the move. His concern about privacy had been eased by Marta's discretion and by the fact that the L-shaped apartment, with the two bedrooms at opposite ends, made it possible for them to feel alone. In any case, Marta was often gone when they awakened and asleep by the time they returned. Their late arrivals did not disturb her, she insisted. The sleeping pills she took for her chronic insomnia made her dead to the world.

Claire, on the other hand, found Marta's flat very conducive to sleep. For some reason she was sleeping more than she ever had and still feeling listless when she awoke. She'd had a notion of improvising a darkroom in a small dressing room equipped with a wash basin, but so far she had done nothing about it. It didn't matter, she told herself, she hadn't come to Paris to work. In her languorous state, the turmoil Marta accepted, even welcomed, into her life, seemed amazing. Claire roused herself and offered to look after the grocery shopping. Marta protested at first, berating herself for being such a poor hostess, but Claire assured her that she enjoyed the morning walk to the outdoor market on rue de la Bretagne. Marta conceded that she, too, had enjoyed the rich variety of the farmers' market when she had a family to cook for. Now, she shopped at the corner supermarket, the Monoprix.

Claire kept a close watch on Marta's routine and tried to be around when Marta was at home. Marta did her best to satisfy Claire's curiosity about the past, offering scraps of stories about her friendship with Dolly. Claire listened carefully, even when the events Marta described were known to her from Dolly's stories. Everything about Dolly interested her: each bit of information, no matter how trivial, might contain a clue pointing her to the truth.

One morning, while Marta was helping herself to a *pain au chocolat* Claire had brought back from the good *boulangerie* in the market, she suddenly broached a theme Claire had never heard Dolly mention. "In one way or another, I always envied Dolly," Marta said, looking at Claire defiantly, as if she had become Dolly's stand-in. "The very first time she brought me home after school — your grandparents lived in a triplex in the shabbier part of Outremont —I wanted her mother. Someone who was there to greet you after school with treats, ready to listen to whatever you had to say. My father and stepmother lived on a much grander scale — thanks to my father's furniture factory in the city's east end — but ours was a cold household. I wanted Dolly's family to adopt me. I certainly spent more time there than I did in my own home. I continued to envy her as we grew up. Externally, I always had more than Dolly: more spending money, more clothes, I was the better student — except in art, of course — the better athlete — if not for me, Dolly would have been chosen last when we selected teams in sports. Yet, I wanted to have what she had. I would have gladly traded my fancy store-bought outfits for the pretty dresses your grandmother made for her. It was the same with boys. I had my fair share of suitors, yet it seemed to me the most desirable boys went for Dolly."

The look of bitterness on Marta's face after so many years surprised Claire. "But Dolly always told me what good friends you were. How inseparable you were growing up."

"Of course she did. She had no idea what I was feeling. She was not given to jealousy herself and so she did not suspect it in others. I resented her for not finding anything to envy about me. I would test her in small, bitchy ways, boasting of my charge accounts and flaunting my extravagant purchases, hoping to upset her. I never succeeded. Even then, Dolly lived in a world of her own."

Claire recognized Marta's distress. She remembered how painful Dolly's self-containment could be for those close to her.

"For all the bragging I did about my family's wealth," Marta continued, "it was Dolly who kept me from starving during my first months in Paris. I could not turn to my family for help because my father had vehemently opposed my move. To make matters worse, before I left I had taken some money he kept in the house. As a Socialist, I believed my father had no right to be as rich as he was. In any case, I told myself I was borrowing against my future inheritance. The money disappeared quickly. I couldn't find work and the little I had went to pay Bruno's fines each time he was arrested at a demonstration. I had to ask your mother to help us. She was then engaged to your father and working as an art teacher. She sent what she could and convinced her fiancé to help as well. I paid them back eventually, but I never forgot Dolly's ready generosity. By that time, I had finally stopped envying her. I was in love with Bruno, I was in love with Paris, and Montréal seemed very insignificant."

Claire was encouraged by the easy flow of Marta's reminiscences. Marta said that having Claire nearby made her remember things she hadn't thought of in years. About Dolly's visits to Paris, however, she had little to say. Asking Marta direct questions was useless. "Why do you always want to talk about old things?" she would respond in all innocence. "What's past is past. Nothing can change that." Yet Marta seemed to need to talk about the past — the segments of it that she chose to highlight — as much as Claire wanted to hear about it. Claire hoped Marta's stories would eventually move forward in time.

When she wasn't listening to Marta, Claire found herself with time on her hands. She hadn't known such idleness in years and the experience was both enjoyable and unsettling. She spent hours wandering the city, seeking out unknown streets and *quartiers*, occasionally taking photographs when something caught her eye, like any of the tourists she passed on her way. Her camera, an instrument of scrutiny in the past, a license to explore what lay partially hidden behind the surface of normality, seemed to have become an extension of her arm rather than her brain; the arm that casually raised the camera to her eye and made it click now and then. When she tired of walking, she found a café and watched the passing scene. The people rushing past her, even the young ones, had the familiar look of big city fatigue, as if just getting about in crowded streets and dense traffic took its toll.

Her own aimless hours also came at a price. She felt herself drifting away from the people around her. Adrian, Marta, Zoé, were all implicated in daily life, attached to it by a multiplicity of obligations insignificant in themselves, which nevertheless anchored them securely and tied them to others. She had escaped, if only temporarily, life's routine claims, but her freedom weighed heavily upon her.

In low moments, she envied Marta's worries about her grandson, Zoé's exhaustion at the end of a day spent listening to her patients, Adrian's growing file of three-by-five cards covered in his fine handwriting. In contrast to their purposeful lives, she floated aimlessly in a gray zone of undefined days where people wandered the streets and sat in cafés staring at others rushing by. She realized to what extent she had always relied on work to give her life a semblance of sanity and order. Left to her own devices, who knew where she would end up? She found it an effort to write the occasional cheerful card she knew her agent Lucinda expected. And as for Dolly, her search had yielded nothing so far. What if her suspicions proved as insubstantial as the ghostlike voice of the philosopher? She turned frequently to Rousseau's writings to steady her nerves, and imagined Dolly's amusement to see her daughter seeking comfort in the works of the teacher she had once mocked.

It didn't help matters that Marta continued her practice of questioning Claire about her daily activities. "Don't you get bored?" she would ask when Claire finished her brief account. Marta's disapproval no longer troubled her as it once had; nevertheless, she was tempted at odd moments to invent a more worthwhile itinerary to please Marta. Nor did Marta approve of Claire's continued reading of Rousseau. "Why would you want to waste your time on a self-declared misogynist? Did you know he excluded women from the education reforms he advocated? Just because Dolly had a strange fascination for the man doesn't mean you have to imitate her." Claire responded by removing her book from Marta's view.

She was reading Rousseau's *La Nouvelle Héloïse* in the Luxembourg garden one day when she saw Marcel heading in her direction. She had looked up from her book to watch children noisily competing for brass rings on the nearby *manège* of wooden horses, and spotted his bulky figure and sidelong loping stride, unmistakable even from a distance. Had she wanted to, Claire could have avoided the meeting, but she found herself welcoming the distraction Marcel was sure to provide.

She was not disappointed. After shaking her hand, Marcel immediately began to complain. "Thank God for this chair. I've just spent the morning at the Beaubourg and I'm ready to drop. Every time I have to go into that strange museum, with its garish insides so indecorously revealed, I suffer an attack of the *mal de Beaubourg*. Don't laugh. It's a well-known condition. Something to do with the electrical wiring not being properly grounded. It hits one in the knees, you see," he said, rubbing his legs.

His eyes fell upon the book beside Claire. "I see you are still interested in the extravagant Swiss barbarian," Marcel said, settling with relief into the chair next to hers. Nervous as ever, he seemed unable to keep his hands still as they moved to loosen his shirt collar, smooth his hair, adjust his glasses. Once he began to speak, his agitation became less noticeable and he used his sonorous voice to advantage.

"I hope my little gift encouraged your interest in Rousseau. He's no longer considered a great novelist, too sentimental and didactic for contemporary tastes. In his time, however, this novel became a powerful force for change." Marcel unraveled his scarf, fidgeted for a while trying to make himself comfortable, and finally continued. "In the mid-eighteenth century when it was considered fashionable to be ironic about passion, to be skeptical of forthrightness, to smile with condescension at women who professed to love their husbands, along came Rousseau, a wild man with wild ideas, exalting passion, love, sentiment, fidelity. At a time when civilized life was lived in over-stuffed rooms and rigorously designed gardens, Rousseau forced the French to open their windows and admire natural landscapes. Paris was the center of the civilized world in Rousseau's time. Yet Rousseau captured the attention of the world with a novel where the main characters reject French civilization and find their happiness not only outside of Paris, but outside France on the distant banks of Lac Leman. It's hard to imagine a contemporary novel having that kind of influence. Of course, Rousseau did not have to compete with the three-minute video clip and other technological marvels."

Marcel's voice rose as he reached the climax of his exposition and Claire noticed that several people had stopped to listen to him. Only in Paris, she thought, could a man draw a small crowd extolling the virtues of an eighteenth-century novel. At moments such as this it was easy to forgive Marcel his excesses.

"There is a rather mean-spirited explanation for the originality of his ideas," Marcel continued, taking no notice of his new listeners. "It suggests that Rousseau's theories derived from a small defect in his physiology. He exalted solitude and country life because of his unfortunate need to piss about two hundred times a day, preferably without being seen. After all, as a young man, when his affliction was less severe, he was drawn to Paris like any other ambitious young provincial of his time. French society, which had elevated intelligent conversation to an art form, must have been very attractive to a man enchanted by words. When necessity forced him into exile, he transformed his condition into a philosophical imperative. Great ideas are often born out of such base necessity, but genius plays its part as well. Few men suffering from urinary problems end up writing a book as magnificent as this one. Would you like me to read out loud some of it to you?"

"Thank you, Marcel, but I really must be going." Unlike Marcel, Claire was very conscious of his audience.

"I've done it again, haven't I?" he said. Fortunately, he had lowered his voice. "My gaucherie never fails to drive women away. You see, I was suddenly struck by the idea that the novel you're reading describes the relationship between an awkward tutor and a beautiful young woman who is forbidden to him. You listened so admirably to my tired ideas about Rousseau, I thought perhaps we could reenact the novel's plot."

Marcel's gallantry meant nothing, Claire knew, it was merely a Frenchman's reflexive response, like opening an umbrella when rain begins to fall. Nevertheless, she felt it marked a détente in their hostilities.

"I really do have to go. Why don't you walk me to the Métro?" she added, feeling free of the constraint that usually came over her in Marcel's presence. Marcel, as soon as he stopped talking, became his usual awkward self. She could see why Adrian felt protective of his friend. Despite his brilliance, Marcel faced each day as if it were a treacherous terrain spiked with insurmountable hurdles. A wild barbarian, like Rousseau, he careened breathlessly from one crisis to the next, leaving behind a trail etched in disappointment. He needed protection from himself, she decided.

Stepping into Adrian's role, she offered him a Métro ticket for his ride home.

As they walked towards the Odéon station, Marcel held forth about Sophie, who was working with him as his research assistant during the summer. He praised her wisdom, astonishing in one so young, her diligence, her dedication. "She's made herself invaluable to me. I don't know what I would do without her."

Why was he trying to convince her of Sophie's virtues? Claire wondered, listening to his effusive praise of his protégée. She had to concentrate, however, on assuring their progress since Marcel felt obliged to pause every time he wanted to make a point, unaware of the pedestrians he forced onto the road by blocking the narrow sidewalk. Claire permitted herself only an occasional murmured assent while she gently nudged him towards their destination.

On the train, she thought of Rousseau's affliction as Marcel had described it and felt a kinship with the philosopher. If Marcel was right, then Rousseau's flights from society were not unlike her own escapes from work, both she and Rousseau undone by bodily treachery. Who better to recognize the pathology of avoidance than a fellow sufferer? No wonder she was beginning to find him sympathetic. She had to tell Zoé of her discovery.

She fell asleep to the rocking of the Métro and awoke to find herself alone in the car at the end of the line. Waiting for a train to take her back, she thought she needed a keeper as well. The persistence of her unusual fatigue worried her. Perhaps Dr. Alvarez had missed something. She would ask Zoé to arrange an appointment with her physician.

ELEVEN

The next morning Claire awoke feeling more energetic and forgot about her fears. When Adrian showed her the photographs he had picked up of their visit to Château de Dormay, she decided to call the countess and take her up on her invitation. The photographs shot in haste from a car window had not turned out well, as Adrian had feared, but they conveyed enough of the dilapidated charm of the place to make Claire wish to see it again. She remembered her desire to photograph the countess and thought the visit, at the very least, would offer the promise of diversion of which she was badly in need. She was getting nowhere with Marta, who continued to evade her questions about Dolly. The frustration of it all was probably what was making her so tired, she decided.

When Claire called, the countess hesitated a moment before recognizing her — it had been two weeks since their brief meeting — and then repeated her invitation with charming insistence. "Come tomorrow. If you plan to visit someone my age, you must not put it off too long. Come early. I have much I want to show you and I'm not at my best late in the day."

Marta took an instant dislike to the countess when she heard about the planned visit. "I can't imagine why you would want to go," she said. "People of that class — *la petite noblesse* — belong to the most backward element in France. You will be bored stiff." Then, revealing a new note of rivalry, she added, "Instead of spending time with some desiccated aristocrat you'd be much better off meeting a few of *my* friends, people who have done something with their lives and who have been a part of the events that shaped this country in the last decades." In fact, it was Marta who had been avoiding Claire — or, rather, her persistent questions — but Claire assured Marta there was nothing she would like better. Nevertheless, early the next morning she took the train specified by the countess, whose name she had learned from the card was Jacqueline de Guersaird.

She was met at the train by Thomas, one of the countess' two elderly servants, who drove her to the château. When the car pulled into the circular driveway she caught sight of the countess de Guersaird waving from one of the windows. The older woman was dressed in the same tight black knitted dress she wore on Claire's last visit, only this time she had added a string of oversized pearls and long turquoise earrings which matched her elaborate eye make-up. Beneath her black hose, Claire noticed, her calves were wrapped in bandages.

"I'm so glad you came, my dear," she said, embracing Claire. "I thought we would have some tea to refresh you from your journey." Her regal hostess led the way into a large room Claire had not seen before. It was nearly bare of furniture but the walls were densely covered with portraits of the countess' ancestors. A decorative molding above the paintings held a display of ornate platters. "This is my private apartment," the countess explained. "I live essentially in three rooms. My son and his family occupy a larger set of rooms in the opposite wing when they're here. The rest of the house is shut up, I'm afraid. Too expensive to maintain."

The Countess de Guersaird continued to speak in excellent, British-accented English, while a maid, as ancient as her mistress, and who turned out to be Thomas' wife, served them tea and slices of plum tart. "These plums come from our garden," she informed Claire. "We allow nothing to go to waste here." On the table between them, half-covered by a cloth of green felt, the countess had spread out albums of her photographs going back nearly seventy years. "I'm almost embarrassed to show them to you," she said, holding out the first of the embossed books after they'd had their tea.

"I love looking at old photographs," Claire said, opening the book with genuine interest. She had always been drawn to family albums, even when the subjects were unknown to her, and from years of scouring flea markets, she had acquired a sizable collection of anonymous amateur snapshots. These casual records conveyed a sense of immediacy often absent in professional work where the personality of the photographer intruded between subject and viewer. Adrian grumbled that she was turning their house into a memorial to the unknown photographer, but he was good-natured about helping her cart home her purchases.

The countess' albums, however, were neither the work of an unskilled amateur nor of a self-conscious stylist. They were in a class of their own. As Claire turned the heavy ornamented pages she realized she was looking at an astonishing chronicle of life lived in a large country house: scenes of hunting, riding, family celebrations, flower-picking, excursions in the woods, wine-making, mushroom-gathering, and countless other activities, all fusing into a cinematic-like depiction of the privileged lives of landed gentry. The countess' photographs, even the very early ones, struck Claire as remarkably direct and immediate. Despite their cuttlefish hues and otherworldly settings, the figures in them appeared to be real flesh-and-blood people. The photographer's lens cut through extravagant costumes and settings to reveal an expression or a gesture that instantly fixed the person in the viewer's mind. There were very few posed pictures or portraits, and seen together, in carefully arranged order, these snapshots represented a fascinating document, devoid of any self-conscious esthetic.

Claire praised the photos with genuine enthusiasm as she turned the pages, but Madame de Guersaird dismissed her words. "I certainly had an eye for things. That is what M. Lartigue told Papa, and I suppose the albums have some historical value now, but I never saw myself as anything other than an amateur who amused herself by keeping a visual diary of what was, after all, a very circumscribed life. I lacked the discipline of the true artist. There must be hundreds of men and women of my time who were equally taken with this new toy, but that didn't make them artists. In a different age, who knows? I might have done something." In response to Claire's admiration, she handed her two views of the house taken in the twenties. "These are for you, a memento of this day."

Claire's attention was caught by a photograph of a group of soldiers lounging on the terrace she had passed earlier. "Germans," the countess explained. "Two hundred and fifty Germans lived here during the war. I was alone with all those *sales boches*. My husband, you see, had been sent to Buchenwald for organizing a Resistance network in the area. When he came back at the end of the war, he weighed forty-four kilos. A walking skeleton. He was never quite the same again." The countess paused to show Claire two photographs of her husband, taken before and after the war, and Claire saw the transformation of a somewhat foppish young man with an open smile into a sad-eyed invalid who reminded her of Marta's Bruno in his last years.

"While he was away," the countess continued, "I carried on his work. Right under the noses of the *boches*. My contact in the Resistance was a man we passed off as a potato merchant. He asked me to collect information on the German defense installations. I had permission from the officer in charge to leave the château grounds. Every day I rode my bicycle through the potato fields where the Germans had hidden anti-aircraft guns and small planes they used for strafing troops and refugees fleeing southward."

She paused again to show Claire a photograph of a smiling young woman on a bicycle dressed in a riding habit. "They took away my horses, but my clothes were of no use to them," she said by way of explanation. "I didn't dare take my camera, so I made drawings and took careful notes in a tiny notebook I kept in my pocket. I passed the information on to my contact, the *faux* potato merchant. Had the Germans found my notebook, I suppose I would have been shot or subjected to something far more unpleasant. Fortunately, I was too busy scheming to feed my starving villagers to worry about myself. The Germans didn't lack for anything, you see, and I became an expert in smuggling supplies from the château. I never again felt as useful as I did during those long months."

Claire thought of Marta, who used almost the same phrase to describe her feelings about the political work she and Bruno had engaged in. She made a note to tell Marta how wrong she had been about Madame de Guersaird.

"It's very dangerous to encourage an old woman to talk about the past," the countess said, rising with some difficulty from her chair. "Come my dear, give me your arm. I want to show you around."

To her surprise, Claire found herself firmly directed by the frail figure towards another cavernous chamber. "This room is dedicated to Diana, goddess of the hunt," the countess explained. "The château was built here because of the great game reserves once found in this area."

The walls, Claire saw, were covered with deer heads and antlers, pheasants, rifles, whips. Between these accoutrements hung photographs of hunting parties setting out on horseback or on foot in pursuit of deer, boar, and wild hare. Here Marta would find justification for her disdain of *la petite noblesse,* Claire thought.

The countess led the way down a curved staircase to a lower level revealing an immense old-fashioned kitchen with a tiled floor where, she explained, hunters had entered with muddy boots to warm themselves and share a drink. She pointed out a corner of the room which had been turned into a modern kitchen. "We had more than two dozen servants working here at one time," she said as they walked around the vast kitchen. "Now, I only keep the two you've met. Life is so much simpler these days, don't you think?"

Claire had noted that the countess' manner with her two helpers remained imperious, as if she were still commanding battalions of domestics, but the ancient couple showed no sign of being in awe of their equally ancient mistress.

"Now we'll take a little drive," the countess said when they found themselves outside. "I want to show you as much of the estate as possible. I will explain my purpose later. But you must make the most of this visit. I'm afraid this property will not outlast me." She showed no trace of melancholy, however, as she drove along narrow country roads, providing Claire with a brisk commentary on the passing scenery.

"What a peaceful corner of the world," Claire said, noting the pristine landscape and the near absence of traffic. "It's hard to believe we're only a couple of hours from Paris."

"These back country roads are lovely, aren't they? But don't let their beauty fool you, the beast strikes here, as easily as anywhere."

Claire turned towards the older woman, unsure of her meaning. "*Le mal*, evil," she explained. "I'm not speaking of war now, when every man turns into a savage ready to destroy his enemy. I was referring to civilian acts of horror. Last year, in a village nearby, a farmer shot his wife, his seven children, his wife's parents, and two of the children's friends who were visiting. Then he turned the gun on himself. People said he was an unremarkable man and asked how could such evil happen here. It reminded me of friends during the war who could not understand how a people as cultivated as the Germans could stoop to acts of such barbarity. I'm afraid neither great culture nor the wonders of nature can keep the beast at bay."

The Countess de Guersaird's remarks were delivered in a matter-of-fact tone, and without pausing, she easily resumed her description of passing landmarks. For Claire, however, the countryside had taken on a more somber aspect.

"We must stop and say hello to the doctor," the countess said when they reached the village. "Country manners are still quite rigid around here."

From what she had seen of Gilbert and his wife, Claire doubted they subscribed to country etiquette, but she said nothing. She already knew her companion well enough not to offer objections.

There were a number of people in the waiting room whom the countess greeted by name. "Is the doctor alone?" she asked the nurse. "Good. We won't keep him," she said, leading the way to Gilbert's office. "I'll only be a moment." No one protested.

They chatted pleasantly with Gilbert until he reminded the countess that she had not kept her last appointment. "My dear doctor," Madame de Guersaird responded, "at my age, there is no good news to be found in a doctor's office. Your machines and your tests can only confirm the decay I see in the mirror every day. Away from mirrors and cameras" — here she looked pointedly at Claire as if reading her intentions — "and from your fine instruments, I can fool myself occasionally. You don't want to deprive me of my illusions, do you? Here," she said, holding out her hand, "you may take my pulse if you wish. Then we will leave you to attend to those people outside for whom you can still do something."

On their way out, Gilbert inquired if Claire had seen Marcel recently. "He's never in, and he doesn't respond to the messages I leave. I hope he's not ill."

Claire assured him Marcel seemed fine only two days earlier, but she noticed Gilbert still looked worried. She suggested he try Sophie, who would know how to reach him.

"I'd prefer not to do that, since I need to talk to Marcel *about* Sophie. She's been acting very strangely and I'm counting on his influence with her."

Claire was happy to repeat all the praise about Sophie she'd heard from Marcel.

"You have an hour until your train leaves," the countess said as they sipped a glass of wine back at the château. "My dear, it's been a terrible day, hasn't it?"

They were now speaking French and Claire looked up in surprise. "I see you don't know that expression. When I was young we used the word *terrible* for everything we enjoyed. Now, there's something I must ask you. Would you do an old woman a great favor? I would like to commission you to photograph the château and its grounds. A sort of final portrait, you might call it. One way or another, this house and I will soon be going our separate ways. In my day, it was customary to have one's portrait taken on the eve of a long voyage or any kind of separation, a souvenir to leave behind for your loved ones. I would like your photographs to be taken in the same spirit. I promise not to interfere. You are not even obliged to talk to me when you come out here next time. You will be as free as you wish."

On the train back to Paris, Claire considered the countess' invitation. While her reputation was based mostly on photographs of people, the idea of photographing the château and its gardens offered intriguing new possibilities. The work would certainly be a change from the usual dense city settings for her portraits. The site itself appealed to her and she was not averse to spending time exploring it. The countess, however, might be a problem. Could she keep her promise not to interfere? She saw again the image of the young chatelaine on her bicycle, her smiling pretty face revealing nothing of the dangers she faced. For all her present fragility, the countess was still capable of imposing her will.

She thought of the frightening symptoms she had experienced at work. She had been fine since her arrival in France, except for feeling unusually tired, but would a new assignment bring them on again? It seemed unlikely. Here, there would be no deadlines, no assistants, no reluctant subjects, no sealed interiors. She pictured herself walking along the carefully laid-out paths of the old estate, camera in hand. The image pleased her and made her think of Dolly. The countess offered her a chance to follow her mother, using her camera the way Dolly had used charcoal. Would Rousseau be her guide as well? Once again, she wished she knew more about Dolly, her thoughts, her special relationship to nature. Why had she taken it all for granted while her mother was alive, never asking the questions that now would never be answered? She closed her eyes and saw Dolly striding ahead of her, intent on her surroundings. Claire was a child again, running after her mother, but hard as she tried, she could not catch up to her mother to see her face.

She turned to the book Marcel had given her and found a passage she remembered on the duplicity of benefactors: "Wealthy patrons have been the bane of my existence," she read. "They are all tact and consideration when courting you, showering you with endless flattery and assurances that they consider you the most important artist alive. But once you agree to become part of their court, the mood changes. They insinuate themselves into your work and proclaim to all their friends that their share in your creation is much greater than you are willing to admit. They inevitably accuse you of being insufficiently grateful. And always, there is the suspicion you are taking advantage of their generosity and wealth. You have to learn to read their moods, to stay out of their way when they are irritable and to be ready to offer amusement, whether you feel like it or not. Above all, you have to know when to leave, before admiration turns to contempt, before freedom gives way to slavishness."

Claire, who had already decided to accept the countess' offer, was not about to change her mind. She'd had enough of Rousseau for the moment and put the book away. She closed her eyes and dozed off, lulled by the rhythm of the train.

TWELVE

"How's the phantom philosopher?" Zoé asked, calling between patients.

"You'll be happy to know I'm ignoring his advice. Perhaps that's the reason I haven't heard from him again."

"Good for you. I'm always encouraging my patients to assert themselves. Listen, I've had a wonderful idea. I'm going to give a dinner party to bring together once again the participants of that magical day at Ermenonville. I hate to see all the good feeling evaporate. Gilbert, Anne-Marie and Sophie were so hospitable to us, it's moved me to reciprocate. It's been ages since Simon and I had people over for dinner. You know, Claire, in all my years of analysis I've not managed to rid myself of this infantile trait that makes me wait for others to initiate my pleasures. But I'm determined to fight it now."

Giving a dinner party was not high on Claire's list of pleasurable activities; she could not understand why anyone would choose to devote time and energy to preparing an elaborate meal when it was so much easier to meet in a restaurant and dispense with the tedious arrangements. Zoé, however, had always enjoyed receiving and serving friends in her home and appeared to do it painlessly. Claire felt she ought to offer her help, inexpert as it was.

"I'm going to keep it so simple, I really won't need any help," Zoé replied. "I won't even think about dinner until Saturday. I'll probably sleep late, have a long bath, read the newspapers. Then I'll walk over to the outdoor market at Carrefour Buci and see what looks tempting. In any case, it won't be anything extravagant. You know how lazy I am."

Zoé was anything but lazy, Claire thought, but she did admire her nonchalance, just as Zoé admired Claire's ease in traveling. Neither felt entitled to admiration for things done without effort.

Zoé had agreed to allow Claire to bring dessert. So now she stood in front of Marta's apartment building, carefully balancing a large pink box containing a *miroir aux framboises* from a *pâtisserie* Marta had recommended, while Adrian hunted for a cab. Marta had insisted on waiting with her. Claire could have done without her company; Marta had been nothing but critical the entire day.

Her dislike of the countess persisted despite Claire's account of the countess' wartime heroism. "Everyone in France of a certain age now claims to have been in the Resistance. It means nothing."

And why had Marta been so caustic about the dinner party as she watched Claire dress? Marta and Zoé had always liked each other, so that wasn't the reason. The idea of the dinner itself seemed to upset Marta, and she expressed this by launching into a long reminiscence about the simple life she and Bruno had led when they were young and working for the betterment of the world. In the process, Marta had criticized the black silk suit Claire wore, the cake she had bought, the champagne Claire had unwisely reported Simon liked to serve, as well as the other guests, whom Claire had described at Marta's own request.

What was it all about? Claire wondered. If Marta felt neglected, then why did she plead lack of time whenever Claire suggested an outing? Was it the idea that her own, often-promised family dinner had yet to materialize? Claire told herself not to take Marta's crabbiness to heart. Marta followed an equal opportunity policy and no one escaped her irritation. She had never been easy to get along with and age had not improved her disposition.

"You certainly know how to show yourself off to advantage," she now said, surveying Claire critically. Somehow, Claire didn't think the remark was meant as a compliment. "At your age, you can still get away with dressing in black and wearing your hair long. But you should start thinking about cutting it. Long hair tends to drag the features down.

And black on older women looks like Sicilian mourning."
Claire was about to mention the countess' preference for
black, but thought better of it.

"You know, you don't really look much like your
mother," Marta went on in the same aggrieved tone,
although she generally claimed the opposite, "except at
certain moments. Tonight, for example. There's an advantage to dying young like Dolly. Bruno and I never saw her
age, and in our memories she remained the age you are
now."

Claire wished Adrian would hurry up. She'd had just
about enough of Marta's carping, focused once more on
Zoé. "Take my advice, Claire, don't confide too much in
Zoé. I know you two are good friends, but friendship is
always tinged with rivalry. Especially between women.
Why give her ammunition to use against you?"

Before she could defend Zoé, Adrian returned with a
taxi he had been lucky to find at Place de la République.
There was a demonstration going on and traffic was in
chaos, he told her. Claire was relieved Marta didn't know
about the protest. She could just hear her grumbling about
people who drank champagne while others marched for a
cause.

They did not reach their destination as early as Claire
had hoped, but she was pleased to see that they were ahead
of the other guests. Simon led them into the living room
where the chilled champagne with its loosened cork waited
to be served.

"I've already had a scotch or two, but I think you should
begin with champagne." Simon was at his best on such
occasions when his natural politeness and love of ceremony
found expression in the role of host. Claire was relieved to
see him in such good spirits. She knew Zoé had been
worried lately about his persistent dejection and his
increased drinking.

"To you, my dear friends," he said, raising his glass, "for coming here and making the party possible. It's been a long time since I looked forward to an evening as much."

Claire took her glass of champagne and went off to the kitchen to deliver the cake and find Zoé. Zoé looked lovely, she thought, discreetly made-up and dressed in a becoming shade of pale green. Claire saw at once, however, that Zoé had been crying. Beneath the unaccustomed green eye shadow, her eyes were red-rimmed and watery.

"What's wrong?" she asked immediately. She was grateful theirs was not the sort of friendship where one had to weigh the wisdom of direct questions.

"Oh, it's nothing serious," Zoé replied, proceeding with her preparations. Claire felt particularly inept as she listened to her friend and watched her hands move efficiently from task to task. "I'm just sick of the constant battling that goes on between Simon and our son. Juliette can do no wrong and Christophe can't do anything right as far as Simon is concerned. This afternoon was a perfect example. Juliette was away, no doubt preparing for some anti-racist demonstration with her friends. God, that child can be deadly serious at times. Of course, it's a reaction against what she perceives to be my frivolous nature. You can't imagine how painful it can be to be watched by a disapproving adolescent."

Claire, who had always liked Juliette, felt compelled to defend her. "Come on Zoé, Juliette admires you. She's just trying to carve out a niche of her own. Remember how single-minded you were about your studies when I met you? Juliette is trying to emulate you in her own way."

"You're right. It's really Christophe I'm worried about. This morning he kindly offered to help me tidy the flat. He's really becoming a very considerate young man, although Simon is probably right in saying he's too attached to me. When Christophe was little, I'm afraid I was not a very good mother. There was the usual anxiety one feels with a first child and I was still in training, caught up in narcissistic preoccupations about my own conflicts with my parents. Here, hand me the colander right next to you. By the way, you look wonderful in that black dress and those sexy high heels. Don't they kill your feet?"

It took Claire a moment to adjust to the shifts in Zoé's conversation. "They're all right," she said after a pause, having finally spotted the colander. "As long as I don't have to walk."

Zoé erupted in a paroxysm of laughter that shook her small frame and produced an unusually loud sound, given her size. In her exuberance, she dropped the morel mushrooms she had just rinsed and they scattered over the kitchen floor. "*Merde,*" she said, getting down on her knees. "At the price I paid, I can't afford to lose a single one." Claire hiked up her skirt and joined her. They were down on all fours when Simon and Adrian walked in.

"Do you need any help, *chérie?*" Simon asked innocently.

Zoé threw one of the prized mushrooms at him. "No, we're managing fine. This is just a little bonding ritual Claire and I do whenever we get together. Gathering food for our men. Now leave us to get on with it."

When the men withdrew, Claire and Zoé were overcome by an unending fit of giggles. They no longer knew why they were laughing, but each found mushroom set them off anew. Claire's attempts to rise, unsteady in her high heels, caused Zoé to collapse again. "You know, Claire," she said leaning her back against a cabinet and wiping her eyes, "it took me years to realize I didn't have to wear high heels, or go to a hairdresser, or be uncomfortable just because I was born female. It was quite liberating. But watch out for Simon. He will probably drool all over you tonight. High-heeled black sandals do strange things to him."

The mention of Simon's name reminded Claire that she still did not know the cause of Zoé's red eyes, looking even redder now without the camouflage of make-up which Zoé had managed to wipe away. "Finish the story," she told Zoé, "before the others arrive."

"Right. Well, as I said, Christophe helped to straighten up the flat. Then he went shopping with me at the market and carried home the heavy bags. When we got back, he made himself a sandwich and ate it in front of the television. That's when Simon emerged from his study, where he had conveniently retired on the pretext that he had to attend to work from the office. Have you ever noticed that work does not provide the same sort of shelter from domestic turmoil for women as for men? I have a male patient, a writer, who has a lot of bizarre habits, but the most shocking thing he ever revealed to me was how absorbed he becomes when he is working. 'If someone were to attack my child while I'm writing, I would eventually become horrified and angry, but at that moment I would wish for the attacker to take her out of earshot so that I wouldn't be disturbed.' I doubt if any woman with a child nearby has ever experienced that degree of absorption.

"In any case, Simon was horrified when he found Christophe eating and watching television. He detests when the TV is on during the day and when the children bring food into the living room. His mother, you know, is an absolute tyrant when it comes to cleanliness, which is why, I suppose, she rarely visits us. Simon proceeded immediately to scold Christophe, who responded by throwing his sandwich at Simon. Christophe then ran out of the house, shouting, 'You see Maman, I can't stay here. He treats me like a child.' Then of course Simon and I had a row and I cried. The tears actually helped; I've had a very tense week. But poor Christophe, he hasn't come back yet. *Voilà,*" Zoé concluded with a note of satisfaction, as she finished decorating the lamb roast with rosemary and garlic and set it in the oven.

"Isn't there anything I can do?" Claire asked, her uselessness weighing heavily upon her.

"I think you'd better stay put in those shoes. In any case, everything is under control. The asparagus is in the steamer. The hollandaise sauce is made. I have a mussel pâté in the fridge. Just before the lamb is done, I'll sauté these mushrooms with some tomatoes and that's it. It's all really very simple."

Claire didn't think there was anything simple about Zoé's dinner. When the other guests gathered around the dining room table set with pale green Limoges china, a green linen tablecloth embroidered with purple peonies, and a dazzling profusion of crystal and silverware, they were equally impressed. Gilbert, Anne-Marie and Sophie were a little subdued by this display of opulence as they sat down in the places Simon indicated. Marcel, on the other hand, beamed as he contemplated the table and the dinner it promised. "How beautiful," he exclaimed. "A perfect still life of harmony and beauty."

"*Merci*, Marcel. What you see here are the remnants of my trousseau. Preposterous as it may seem, these trappings were standard equipment for a young girl from a good family in Oran, where I grew up, and where old social customs lingered longer than in Metropolitan France."

"Another erotic practice gone forever," Marcel said with a sigh as he helped himself to asparagus and paté.

"Erotic? What on earth is erotic about a trousseau?" Sophie asked, looking very grown up in an upswept hairdo and a flattering pantsuit.

"Everything." Marcel responded with a dreamy look on his face. "The word itself evokes abundance, as well as blushing innocence, pudency, locked doorways that give way to ornate keys. You know, as in a trousseau of keys."

"I'm afraid all it evokes for me," Sophie said in her even voice, "is a trussed chicken on a spit, you know, as in *troussé*."

"My dear Sophie, you are displaying a regrettable lack of imagination," Marcel responded. "As your teacher, I am deeply disappointed."

Sophie smiled and attended to her long, pale tendrils escaping from the clip which held her hair up. Marcel followed her languid movements with adoring eyes. Could there be anything going on between Marcel and his former student? Claire wondered. Sophie appeared far less docile than in Ermenonville where Claire had last seen her with Marcel. But the look on Gilbert's face told Claire that he was not too happy with his daughter's new-found independence.

Her mother, in the meantime, pursued the argument with unusual sharpness. "The dowry is really a barbaric, demeaning custom. And dangerous as well. I have accompanied Gilbert to India where young brides are sometimes killed if their dowry has not been paid in full. I'm afraid I don't see anything romantic about this practice."

"Strictly speaking," Simon interjected while refilling their glasses, "a dowry and trousseau are quite distinct. Zoé came to me equipped not only with a magnificent trousseau, part of which is spread before you on this table, but her father also insisted on making a marriage settlement. At the time, I was appalled at the suggestion that I become involved in such a mercenary procedure. It was bad enough that I had to participate in an elaborate white wedding at the Hôtel Lutécia, a bourgeois ritual I despised, along with other young men my age. But a financial arrangement, I felt, was an insult to the purity of my feelings for Zoé. I met her father's suggestion with a great deal of indignation. Zoé's father, an estimable gentleman whom I came to admire immensely, listened patiently to my self-righteous sputtering.

"'I didn't mean to insult you,' he assured me with more respect than I deserved. 'I merely wanted to provide my daughter with some degree of comfort in her new life.' To which I, with my beginner's civil service salary, barely permitting me to survive, much less maintain a wife, replied that henceforth I would be the one to see to his daughter's comfort. How well I understand him now that I am the father of a daughter. There's something to be said for the old ways."

"Whenever Simon's had too much to drink," Zoé said laughing, "he becomes nostalgic about the *ancien régime.*"

"Well my darling," Simon replied gravely, "there's good reason to be nostalgic. Your father, through his prudence and generosity, was able to provide his children with a start in life. What will we pass on to our children? I'm afraid we have been far more extravagant and selfish than our parents, and our children will suffer for it."

"Oh Lord, please stop him," Zoé said, giving Claire a look of appeal as she left the table. She returned a minute later, carrying two silk garments. "*Voilà*, Marcel. The erotic part of my trousseau," she said holding up two diaphanous shifts. "I was provided with a dozen similar nightgowns, all made by hand, embroidered and trimmed with old lace. I don't know what's happened to the others but I can still see the dressmakers who worked for weeks preparing my trousseau. Two spinster ladies who did absolutely beautiful needlework. Of course, in the women's quarters, where all this work went on in preparation for my wedding, no one ever mentioned what I was supposed to do once I actually wore one of these sexy garments. In any case, it would have been too late. Simon and I were already living together months before the wedding."

Claire rose to examine the nightgowns more closely. They really were exquisite, she thought, exquisite enough to display on walls. That's where they belonged, she decided on impulse. Taking them from Zoé, she proceeded to suspend them by their straps from the frames of two paintings hanging on opposite sides of the room. A slight breeze wafting in through the windows rippled the gowns and made them sway gently to and fro like dancing figures, exuding the musty scent of sachet and disuse.

"How wonderful and surreal," Marcel said, contemplating the image of the floating gowns headed by the partially obscured figures in the paintings from which they were suspended. "What an imaginative thing to do. You've changed the entire look of the room."

Claire was not used to receiving compliments from Marcel and looked at him with suspicion; his enthusiasm, she thought, was a little excessive. Adrian, however, was delighted with his friend's praise for his wife. "You're right. Claire has a very original way of seeing things. She gets it from her mother, who was a fine artist."

"How I envy you," Marcel sighed. "My own mother believes the fate of civilization depends on the strict observance of social conventions. She has no use for me and suffers my visits with ill-concealed impatience."

Claire remembered how she had longed for a conventional mother, but said nothing. On cue, she heard Zoé say, "Everyone fantasizes about having different parents. Wanting to trade in one's parents is a universal, adolescent rite of passage. At your age, Marcel, you're supposed to have come to terms with the parents you do have. You know, move past the Oedipal phase."

Marcel, encouraged by Zoé's teasing, proceeded to elaborate on his difficulties with his mother, while Gilbert turned to Claire to inquire how she was getting on with the countess. They were quietly comparing notes about her many estimable qualities when they became aware of a heated conversation taking place, dominated by Simon's rising voice. The discussion must have moved from parents to politics. Little else roused such intense feelings in Simon. Claire had no idea how it began but she was dismayed to see how quickly Simon's good humor vanished. She had an inkling now of what Zoé meant when she complained about Simon's alarming mood swings.

Zoé felt that Simon's anger had more to do with the recent disappointments he had suffered than with politics. "He doesn't enjoy his work any longer," she had explained to Claire. "At home, he's always at odds with his son and now his book on Stendhal has been rejected by the few publishers he's tried. You see, he's worked on it off and on for twenty years. Simon's always identified with Stendhal — a diplomat by day, a man of letters by night. Now, all he can look forward to, he says, is a golden handshake and a Légion d'Honneur rosette. Frankly, I'm exhausted from trying to cheer him up."

Claire, who had always liked Simon, sympathized with his difficulties. But as she watched him now, his face flushed, his voice overriding the views of his guests while he pursued some private grievance, she understood Zoé's increasing exasperation with her husband. Claire realized she had to stop Simon; his loss of control threatened her own equilibrium.

She racked her brain for something to say that would divert attention from Simon.

"Did you hear about the man who died in a S&M brothel?" she blurted out in desperation. The incident was true enough — she had read about it in the morning *Herald Tribune*, but her way of introducing it had been less than graceful.

For a moment there was a stunned silence until Marcel, bless his soul, came to her rescue. "Yes, that's quite a story. Did you notice that the dominatrix was German? A descendant perhaps of some concentration camp commander? Apparently, the equipment in her dungeon outstripped anything the Marquis de Sade had ever imagined. I understand she recruited clients through her website. And she wasn't cheap. Her customers had to pay dearly for the pleasure of being tortured. The victim you speak of, Claire, was a prominent lawyer."

"Human nature is baffling, isn't it?" Gilbert said. "In the course of my work with Doctors Without Borders, I've had occasion to treat victims of torture, a practice not restricted to Germans, I assure you, Marcel. I would have a very difficult time explaining to any of these unfortunate creatures the notion of paying for the pleasure of being subjected to pain. I wonder if the element of choice makes the difference."

"Apparently it does," Zoé responded. "Several studies I've read demonstrate that when cancer patients control the amount of pain relief they receive, they can get by with less medication than when the control is in the hands of their physicians or nurses."

"This conversation is far too grim for me," Marcel complained. "Claire's story is about sex, weird as it may be. The search for pleasure is all too often ludicrous, even when it doesn't involve chains, whips, and electric prods. Can any of us say he or she has never behaved foolishly in love? I confess my own amorous adventures have often ended in abject humiliation."

Claire's ploy had worked. By the time the table was being cleared for dessert, Simon appeared ready to join the general banter. When his son returned sometime near midnight, Simon put a friendly arm around his shoulder and proudly introduced him to the new guests. Zoé and Claire's eyes met above the boy's head and they smiled, sharing the pleasure of this brief lull in the struggle between father and son.

Christophe remained wary at first as he watched the merriment around the table, but once Marcel began to speak, he became fascinated. And Marcel, sensing a fresh audience, directed his remarks to the boy, who soon rewarded him with appreciative laughter. Sophie, scarcely older than Christophe, kept her eyes on Marcel as well, smiling fondly at her professor's performance. Claire noticed that Marcel shed some of his most irritating mannerisms with these young admirers.

The evening was going well again and Claire felt herself overtaken by a pleasant, relaxed state of drowsiness. Conversation swirled around her, lapping at the edges of her attention and drifting away. She watched the nightgowns fluttering in the late spring breeze and noted with satisfaction that Simon, Christophe, and Zoé appeared reconciled for the moment. Simon's hopes for the evening had not gone unrewarded, after all.

"Nice to see you relaxed for a change," she heard Adrian whisper in her ear. He was right. It was a relief to be away for a few hours from her frustrations with Marta. Her decision to take up the countess' offer promised a longer respite. She would act on it tomorrow, she told herself, anticipating with pleasure her exploration of the magnificent old estate. She hoped Marta's humor would improve as well if they were apart for a few days.

THIRTEEN

The following morning, however, Claire awakened late, feeling listless and vaguely nauseated. Getting out of bed and calling the countess de Guersaird seemed an immense effort. So she continued to lie there taking stock of her symptoms, as if her body had become an unpredictable alien entity to be approached with caution.

Suddenly, something Zoé had said the previous evening cut through her torpor, causing instant alertness. Their exchange had taken place when Claire, heading for the bathroom, ran into Zoé returning to the dining room with a cheese platter in one hand and a basket of *pain Poilâne* in the other. "Are you all right?" Zoé asked, looking at Claire appraisingly. "You're not feeling panicky or anything?" Zoé knew, of course, about the unnerving symptoms she had experienced.

"I'm fine," Claire reassured her.

"Hm," she said, not convinced, "In that case you're either pregnant or suffering from a shrinking bladder. I've lost count of how many times you've left the table tonight."

Claire had laughed off Zoé's remark, but now the word "pregnant" came sailing towards her like a giant bird heading for its prey, its beating wings echoed in the pounding of her heart.

Was it possible? she wondered after she had calmed down a bit. She had missed a period; but then her cycle had not been regular since she had gone off the pill several months earlier, thinking her fluctuating emotions might be linked to the daily hormone cocktail she swallowed. But she had been using other methods, carefully, conscientiously. It was no use guessing, she decided; she had to know, the sooner the better.

She dressed quickly and left the apartment to buy a pregnancy kit. Neither Adrian nor Marta were about, she noted with relief on her way out. She headed for a large pharmacy on the busy Place de la République. Inside, she panicked for a moment, unable to think of the word for pregnancy in French. When she finally asked for a *test de grossesse*, she was dismayed to be offered a choice of kits, all promising 99% accuracy and quick results. Somehow this was not an area in which she wanted choice; one option would have been far more reassuring.

The flat was still empty when she returned and she hastened to the bathroom, locking the door behind her. The instructions were simple enough: collect urine, insert the testing stick half-way, remove it, place it on a dry surface, and wait two minutes. Two lines on the stick indicated a positive result, one line a negative one.

Claire sat on the edge of the bathtub, keeping track of time with her wristwatch, her mind blank as she concentrated on the circular path of the second hand, ticking inexorably towards her fate. She gave the test an extra minute for good measure and held up the stick to the light to read its message. The stick before her was a perfect match for the illustration in the instruction pamphlet. There were two distinct lines where three minutes earlier there had been none. She was pregnant.

She felt numb as she removed all evidence of the test kit. Was she happy, unhappy, frightened, elated? It was too soon to tell. Her emotions had been flattened by the sheer magnitude of the discovery she had just made. Suddenly her mind flashed to Adrian. She wanted to run out and tell him the news, but she stopped herself. Adrian, she remembered, was bound to be less than overjoyed. She could not bear to hear his well-reasoned objections, not right now, when she was so uncertain of her own feelings. She had never been good with surprises: she needed time to get used to the idea of a baby, to let it settle in her mind as firmly as the embryo was now lodged in her body before she attempted to persuade Adrian.

It was then that she remembered the countess. The best thing she could do, she felt, would be to stick to her plan and get away for a few days. She would take herself and her new secret to the deserted *allées* of the countess' gardens where there would be little to distract her from the thinking she needed to do. Paris was becoming more crowded each day as the ranks of tourists swelled with visitors from Eastern and Central Europe, arriving in busloads to gaze at sites once forbidden to them. The unusually warm weather made her long for shady paths and cool breezes. Within an hour, she was on a train moving swiftly past the desolate grayness of the suburban *périphérique* and into the verdant countryside.

Madame de Guersaird greeted her warmly, and true to her word, stayed out of her way. "I trust you, my dear," she had said to Claire at the outset. "Whenever you think the portrait is complete, I will be happy to take possession of it. Take your time, there's no rush."

During the next few days, Claire explored the park, photographing at random whatever caught her eye, the thought of the baby flitting in and out of her mind. When she forgot about it for a short while, carried away by something she saw, and then remembered again with a start the life growing inside her, she imagined it as a steady beacon, quietly signaling its presence. It was a comforting image, allowing her to concentrate on her work, knowing its beam functioned free of her volition.

The park appeared more magnificent with each visit, its beauty revealed anew whenever the weather or the light changed. She was surprised by the intensity of her response to these woods, flowering prairies and overgrown paths. Unlike Dolly, she did not approach nature as sacred ground, imbued with mystical, creative forces. She had always found her inspiration in the small details and minute artifices that defined the changing landscape of the human face and body. Nor did she feel that nature had to remain untouched and that to alter it was an act of sacrilege. For her own pleasure, she preferred domesticated landscapes to pristine wilderness. The dimensions of her small garden in Montréal, where she spent hours rooting around in the soil, exploring the mysteries of tubers, corms, rhizomes, slips and seeds, observing the struggle for supremacy between different plant species, and the interplay between floral plants and their insect predators, satisfied any yearning she had for the natural world.

The grounds surrounding Château de Dormay represented a happy fusion of nature and artifice, blended to form a stable if ever-changing universe, inviting contemplation and reverie. The vastness of the gardens, their general air of neglect, created an illusion of wilderness and desolation so convincing at times that it startled Claire whenever she came across traces of the original grand plan: a long, tree-lined avenue, suddenly revealing the distant château; a lake framing the reflection of a well-placed statue, its outline blurred by time. These unexpected discoveries made her reach for her camera, excitement quickening her pulse as if she had sighted some rare species which might vanish at any moment. This was what she liked best about the park, she decided, the way it portrayed nature filtered through the human eye, shaped by the human hand, and resonant with history.

The countess had made her aware that this serene landscape had been a fierce battleground during the last war and long before it. The land had been trampled, ravaged, soaked in blood. But when Claire tried to imagine the partisans, the fleeing refugees, the occupying forces she had heard the countess describe, her imagination failed her. The landscape acted like a giant blotter, absorbing all the carnage that had spilled across it and revealing nothing but its smooth green surface.

She was always surprised to see how close the park was to the nearby expressway with its rushing traffic. Overhead, she often heard the sound of jets; the airport was only forty kilometers away. The greenery screened out the road and its noise as well. The nearness of the expressway and the airport made the park seem more vivid each time she entered it— another shrinking patch of resistance — and for how long?

Dormay exerted a strong, calming effect upon her. She felt soothed as soon as she passed through its gates. After a few hours of walking she often felt so drowsy, she had to lie down wherever she was and close her eyes. She awakened from these short naps disoriented, disheveled, and yet wonderfully refreshed. Occasionally, she ran across other people — workmen tending the grounds, villagers taking a short-cut, lovers hidden in the tall grass — who would greet her politely without ever intruding on her privacy. It was as if everyone she met conspired to preserve the solitary enjoyment they came here to find.

She often thought of Dolly, trying to see the landscape through her artist's eye. Whenever she reached for her camera, she heard the scratch of Dolly's charcoal swiftly moving across paper as she captured in a few deft strokes the shape of a boulder or the twisted branch of a tree. How well she understood Dolly's need to escape into the countryside now that she herself had fallen under the charm of these grounds.

Her wanderings were shadowed by invisible presences — her young mother, the unformed baby, the old philosopher — linked through her consciousness, like figures in a dance. Rousseau's writings accompanied her reveries when she tired of walking, his words as much a part of the landscape as the grove of linden trees where she sat reading:

"The useless agitation of the brain turns man into the most unhappy of all animals. Only one activity has ever brought me relief from the demons of despair, the solitary contemplation of nature. Wandering alone through fields, forests, along the shores of lakes and rivers, far from the turbulence of society, I soon forgot the persecution I had experienced at the hands of others, their hatred, their contempt, the treacherous ways they repaid my kindness. Instead, I invented imaginary worlds where friends were loyal, women tender, and merit rewarded. Solitude and nature became my greatest teachers."

Claire did not suffer from the sense of persecution that pervaded the old man's *Confessions*, but her own troubling thoughts became less insistent in the peaceful solitude of the countess' gardens. After a while, she found that simply imagining herself wandering along the meandering paths of the park sufficed to calm her when she needed calming. In a postcard to Lucinda she wrote, "I think I've found my own version of your ashram. Photos to follow."

She described her experience to Zoé in more detail. Zoé said Claire had stumbled on a key technique of relaxation, one she used with patients: encouraging them to focus on a single soothing image that blocked out unwanted mental agitation. Increasingly, as nature itself became imperiled, scenes of natural beauty became metaphors for the redemption of troubled souls. Zoé's patients found comfort in visualizing tumbling waterfalls, waves pounding the shore, fields of wildflowers set in motion by a gentle breeze. The technique usually required practice, Zoé said, but she hoped Claire didn't intend to spend all her time at Château de Dormay.

"You're never around anymore," Zoé complained at the end of their conversation, "and when you are, you seem unusually preoccupied. Is it the new work?"

Claire evaded Zoé's questions. She did not want to say anything until she had spoken to Adrian.

Marta's humor had not improved and Claire's absences merely provided new ground for expressing her disapproval. "I can't imagine why you would want to traipse out to the country all the time, when there is so much to do and see in Paris," she repeated each time Claire announced she would be gone for the day.

Only Adrian, busy with his research, was pleased Claire had found something to do so that he needn't worry about her during the longs hours he devoted to his work. He had a new concern which he confided to Claire one morning as she was preparing to leave for the country: the ever-faithful Marcel had vanished and Adrian was unable to track him down. Messages left at his usual haunts had not been answered and Adrian was at a loss to explain Marcel's unusual silence.

Claire agreed this was strange behavior for Marcel, usually so persistent in his attentions to Adrian. "Maybe you've been replaced by a new object of admiration," she teased him.

"I don't mind, if that's the case," he responded good-naturedly. "I'm just worried he's in crisis again. Marcel has a talent for getting into trouble."

"Then you're bound to hear from him," she said and proceeded to tell him how Gilbert, Sophie's father, had complained of similar difficulties in trying to reach Marcel. "I suspect he enjoys having people wonder what's become of him." Her parting embrace was particularly affectionate, as if to make up for the turmoil she knew she was about to unleash.

Nearly a week had passed since Claire had learned of her pregnancy. The solitude of the countryside, acting like a balm on her spirit, had restored her calmness and given her new strength, despite recurring bouts of fatigue. But she was not ready to share her news. It made her feel closer to the baby to think she was the only person in the world who knew of its existence, the only one sheltering it from harm. Her silence created a fragile covenant of intimacy, too fragile to endure exposure. Another few days, she told herself, and she would be ready to tackle Adrian.

FOURTEEN

The next morning Claire awoke to the sound of heavy rain, forcing her to cancel her trip to Dormay. She decided to spend the day with Marta, but Marta, of course, found reasons to discourage Claire from accompanying her. "You'll be bored stiff. I have nothing but tedious errands ahead of me." Claire restrained herself from pointing out how capricious Marta was being.

Once they were inside Marta's small Renault, however, Marta seemed glad of her presence. For one thing, Claire provided a useful service merely by sitting in the car and warding off a ticket whenever Marta double-parked. Marta told her she was an angel as the morning wore on and they proceeded from one place to another.

Claire didn't mind waiting for Marta. She found herself remembering a day spent with Marta, Bruno and their daughter, Louise, when they had traveled in an equally small car to Chartres to visit its celebrated Cathedral. It had been a cold gray day and after a perfunctory tour of the Cathedral — Marta had said the massive Gothic church, dominating the town as it did, always depressed her — they had happily retired to a nearby restaurant to escape the chill. Marta and her daughter were bickering, as they often did, and Claire no longer remembered what had set them off. But she did remember that she had been stricken with jealousy as she watched the exchange between mother and daughter. The intensity of their involvement with one another left her feeling uncomfortably like an intruder who had no right to witness such an intimate family scene.

Claire hadn't allowed herself to miss her mother. She had decided early on there would no room for mourning in the exciting life she was determined to have. Seeing Marta and Louise engaged in heated opposition, their faces

133

flushed with emotion and focused only on each other, she found herself suddenly on the verge of tears. At that moment in the restaurant Claire desperately wanted Marta to scold her and love her the way she loved and scolded her daughter. She had been forced to run off to the washroom to hide her tears before she made a fool of herself. Waiting for Marta in her car, years later, Claire could still remember how alone she had felt that day. She smiled now, thinking that her visits with a frail aristocrat had finally earned her the scolding from Marta she had once desired.

Her errands done for the morning, Marta decided to stop for a moment at her friend Gertrude's place. "Gertrude would love to see you again," Marta said as she maneuvered the Renault through the dense Paris traffic. "She knew your mother and she remembers meeting you on several occasions. She always asks after you."

But Gertrude, it turned out, was far too depressed to pay any attention to Claire. After a listless greeting, she led her guests to a window overlooking the inner courtyard. "There he is," she said pointing to a man below busily sweeping the pavement. "That's Jacques, my husband," she told Claire.

"What a strange disease Alzheimer's is," Marta said. "Jacques, for example, seems to be comfortable only outdoors. But Gertrude can't very well allow him to wander the streets by himself. He would be lost in no time. So she takes him down to the courtyard where the *concièrge* keeps an eye on him. Lately, he hasn't even tried to escape. He finds so many ways of busying himself."

"I know he's safe," Gertrude continued, "but I can't keep myself from watching him through the window. He's been ill for several years, and I still can't get used to the idea that this man who had one of the most brilliant minds I've ever encountered spends his time compulsively cleaning the courtyard. Has Marta described to you what he does? He can hardly wait for me to dress him in the morning so that he can get out there and get back to his tasks. Sometimes, when it's cold or raining, and I try to keep him indoors, he becomes very agitated. So I let him go and watch helplessly as he cleans the courtyard of every pebble, leaf and piece of dirt he finds. Once it's spotless, he begins to arrange the pile of refuse into neat, intricate patterns. He allows me to lead him back upstairs only when it gets dark. To tell you the truth, when I wake up these days and think of what lies ahead, I wish I were dead. But who would look after him?"

On the way out, Marta insisted on saying hello to her old friend. "He seems pleased to see me whenever I come," Marta said as they descended the stairs. "I think he recognizes me. *Bonjour*, Jacques," she called out across the courtyard. Indeed, her friend set aside his broom and greeted her with a wave and a smile. "Are you going to Montpellier?" he asked eagerly as they drew near.

"Not today, Jacques," Marta replied gently, and he turned away to resume his sweeping. "His son lives there," Marta explained. "He asks the same question every time I see him."

Before they left, Marta asked Claire to take Jacques' picture. "I've been looking through old photographs and I can't find any of Jacques. I'm being silly, I know, but it would please me to have a souvenir of him." She carefully smoothed Jacques' hair, straightened his scarf and told him to smile. Surprisingly, he cooperated.

Claire looked up and saw Gertrude watching at her window. She waved to her, but there was no response. When they were leaving, Jacques politely lifted his hat as they bid him good-bye. "His good manners are the only thing left of the man I knew," Marta said, wiping away a tear. "The ravages of old age are sometimes more painful to bear in one's friends than in oneself."

"I'm so glad I have an appointment with my hairdresser today," she added when they emerged from the courtyard. "After this, I need something to boost my morale." The two women agreed to meet later at Marta's favorite café on rue de Medicis, opposite the Luxembourg garden.

Claire walked to the café. The day had lightened considerably and she looked forward to a good long walk after being cooped up for much of the morning in Marta's car. She needed the time to formulate the questions she intended to ask Marta when they met.

FIFTEEN

Claire made her way slowly along the crowded Paris streets, thinking about Dolly. As far back as Claire could remember, she had been aware that Dolly was unlike the mothers of her friends. When she helped out on school trips, made costumes for school plays, baked cookies for school raffles, doing all the things other mothers did, Claire felt that Dolly was only playing the part of the good mother. The occasional distant expression and the way she had of holding herself as if perched for flight — these gave her away. The truth was that Dolly, unlike other mothers, was usually biding her time until she could return to the waiting forms in her attic studio.

Claire remembered the day she first became aware of Dolly's other existence. It happened during a lengthy bout of bronchitis that kept her away from school. Bored and not really sick enough to enjoy her bed, she wandered up the stairs to find her mother. She had to call out before her mother turned towards her. The face Claire saw then had the blurred, glazed look of a person startled out of a deep sleep. In a moment, a smile of recognition restored the familiar features, but Claire sensed her mother's eagerness to return to her work and to that other self which recognized no external claims.

Claire understood that the mother she had accepted as part of the immutable background of her childhood — the familiar figure whose scent was as intimate as the touch of her own skin, the mother who brushed and braided her hair, who made her daily return from school a special celebration, and presided cheerfully over the dinner table — had a secret other life which neither she nor her father shared.

Although Dolly never scolded Claire for interrupting, Claire knew the strange forms emerging from blocks of wood were formidable rivals for her mother's attention. Despite Dolly's attempts to make her welcome — Claire had her own little table in the studio with pads of paper, crayons, modeling clay, all provided for her amusement — Claire decided she hated everything having to do with art.

Claire was at first delighted when Dolly began to avoid her studio after her return from Paris. Once again there were regular meals, clean laundry, and special treats after school, but the distant look she had seen on her mother's face in the studio became a permanent blankness. Her mother seemed more lost to her than ever. Claire had blamed herself, as if her resentment of her mother's work had caused Dolly to abandon it. She knew now that she was not to blame. Dolly's suffering had been caused by something far more serious than a child's selfishness.

What a conventional child she had been, Claire thought with some remorse, remembering her fierce attachment to Dolly. She could sympathize now both with the child and the mother. Were their needs really so irreconcilable? Would her love for her unborn child, just beginning to bud, prove more reassuring, or would her child judge her as harshly as she had judged Dolly? These sobering questions made it more urgent for her to understand Dolly's unhappiness.

Claire was pleased to see that there was no sign of Marta when she arrived at the café. Marta did not like to be kept waiting and Claire did not want to irritate her on a day when she needed her cooperation.

Her heart sank when Marta joined her and began immediately to search for her keys and eyeglasses. These familiar signs of distress did not bode well. She suspected Marta's agitation had something to do with her new short haircut, tinted an unfamiliar shade of auburn. Before she could say anything, Marta suggested they change tables. "Do you really want to stay here? I think we'd be better off in one of the booths inside."

"I've just made an utter fool of myself," Marta said after they had made the move with the help of a surly waiter. "As you know, I've been going to the same hairdresser for years. I believe I sent you to him when you first came to Paris. He did wonders for you. Naturally, I have come to depend on his advice. So, when he suggested a new rinse today, I agreed. You see, I haven't been able to put anything in my hair since I developed an allergy to hair coloring. I was tempted to try something which would make me look less like a little old lady."

Claire laughed at Marta's description of herself. No matter how old Marta became, Claire doubted anyone would ever see her as a "little old lady."

"You may well laugh. The vanities of aging are more absurd than the self-conscious awkwardness of youth. As one gets older, one becomes obsessed with the bodily functions youth takes for granted. It's like a clock that draws your attention only when it slows down or becomes erratic. In any case, there I was with my new hairdo, happily boarding the Métro to meet you, when a young girl rose to give me her seat. Instead of accepting her offer graciously, in a manner befitting a woman my age, to my horror I found myself berating the girl: 'Do I really look so old and frail, *Mademoiselle*, that you feel you must give me your seat?' You see, Armand had convinced me I would look years younger with my hair tinted. How one grasps at straws. I wish you could have seen the face of that young girl. I'm sure it will be some time before she offers her seat again to anyone on the Métro."

Claire laughed again, and this time Marta joined her. Her confession appeared to relieve her distress and she was herself again. After they had given their orders to the waiter, Claire remembered her resolve. She decided to move slowly towards her target. "I know you don't like my visits to the Countess de Guersaird, but I've been having a wonderful time wandering alone through the vast park. It's made me feel closer to Dolly, for one thing. You remember how happy she was roaming the woods with her sketchbook? I can easily imagine her in that setting."

"I'm glad you're enjoying yourself, but you're mistaken about Dolly," Marta said firmly. " She had no use for the mannered formality of the grand French garden. Her preferences ran to rugged hilly landscapes, like the Laurentians, north of Montréal, where she spent so much time."

Marta was wrong about the grounds at Dormay, where nature was slowly eroding all traces of the original classical plan, but Claire decided to pursue another tack. "The French countryside has made me appreciate Rousseau in a new way. I wish I hadn't been such a brat whenever she talked to me about his teachings. I even made fun of her with my friends. I wasn't a very understanding daughter."

Marta leaned over and patted her hand. "Don't be so hard on yourself. You mother's adoration of Rousseau could be very tiresome at times. She got that from her teacher, I'm afraid. The man who taught her sculpture, I can't think of his name, but I know he urged her to read Rousseau's writings on nature. She credited these writings with some kind of breakthrough in her work. Rousseau became a crutch, a superstition she clung to, believing him responsible for her creativity. As you know, I'm not a fan of Rousseau's misogynist views. Of course there was no discussing him with Dolly. She shared with her mentor an extremely hypersensitive nature — so thin-skinned that at times she seemed to have no skin."

Claire was tempted to tell Marta that Rousseau adored women, but she decided instead to pick up on something Marta had just said. "I don't remember Dolly being that fragile. I always saw her as a very determined and strong-willed person."

"She was," Marta agreed, "but she could be hypersensitive as well. There were some subjects, like Rousseau, for example, where she would not be challenged. Her degree of response, both positive and negative, seemed at times out of proportion. I suppose she possessed what's called an artistic temperament. A mixed blessing, I'm afraid. Thank God you have some of your father's solidness to balance that." Once again Claire was grateful she had not told Marta about her irrational episodes of panic.

"Maybe that explains her depression following her last trip here," she said with hesitation, moving cautiously towards her goal. "Do you think she was simply overreacting to some small disappointment? Or perhaps . . ."

"Surely you're not still going on about that?" Marta interrupted in an angry voice. "God, you're a stubborn girl. Yes, Dolly and I were close, but that doesn't mean we told each other everything. Dolly, like everyone else, had her secrets. I don't believe in turning friendship into a confessional. I warned you about that the other day."

"Please don't be upset, Marta, this is very important to me."

"It's very childish of you to think that everyone's keeping things from you. Anyway, your mother was not the first woman to get sidetracked. Women have never found it easy to be single-minded about work. The life of the emotions distracts us too easily. It's the way we're made or brought up, depending on whom you want to believe. I'm not saying this was the case with Dolly, but it might have been. As I told you before, she would have come out of it eventually if not for the accident."

Claire tried again. "As far as you know, then, her stay in Paris was uneventful."

"What are you hoping to hear?" Marta asked, not bothering to keep the exasperation out of her voice. "All I know is that your questions are giving me an awful headache. I hope you don't torment Adrian this way. Have you talked to him about having a child? Instead of running off to see the countess, you would do better to spend some time with your husband. Don't tell me he's busy. A woman can always get a man's attention, if she wants to."

Marta had not lost her touch, Claire noted, somewhat shaken. Her fairy godmother still had the power to turn herself into a cruel witch.

SIXTEEN

"I'm certain Marta is hiding something," Claire told Zoé the following day. It was still raining and Claire had given in to Zoé and agreed to accompany her to the oriental baths. Zoé had been extolling the wonders of her *hammam* since Claire had arrived. "It's absolutely sybaritic, Claire. The heat, the nudity, the indolence, the pampering, you must come. I don't think I could survive without my weekly visit."

Claire had her doubts about the charms of Turkish baths. She disliked intense heat and vigorous massage, and group nudity made her uncomfortable. She was fond enough of her own body but she had no desire to parade it before strangers, or Zoé, for that matter. She was not ready to share her secret with her friend. But Zoé was feeling neglected and Claire wanted to please her. They hadn't seen each other in a while and Claire missed the quick understanding they shared when they were together. Lately, Zoé had sounded unusually subdued whenever she called between patients, but there had been no opportunity to question her during these brief, rushed exchanges.

The baths were in the Arab quarter, not far from Marta's apartment. Here the rush of cars gave way to dense throngs of people moving slowly through streets transformed into a huge oriental bazaar. Women in djellabas, turbaned old men, children running wild between the feet of adults, crowded the sidewalks where merchants hawked wares ranging from the latest electronic equipment to hanging carcasses of sheep and brightly colored, redolent sacks of spices. Exchanges were shouted rather than spoken, creating a din which, along with the human density, caused Claire to stop frequently. Following Zoé's instructions, she located the building which housed the baths at the end of a twisting maze of alleys. Its exterior was indistinguishable from the dusty tenements surrounding it.

She was glad to find Zoé waiting in front of the arched doorway, excited at the prospect of introducing Claire to the pleasures hidden behind the unassuming façade. With her sparkling eyes and flushed cheeks, she appeared as young as when Claire had first seen her, despite the sober dark suit and the heavy briefcase. "No time to change. I've come straight from work," Zoé explained, following her friend's gaze, and threw her arms around Claire. They hugged happily as if they hadn't seen each other in months. "I've missed you," they uttered in unison and burst out laughing.

"Isn't this area wonderful?" Zoé asked once they were inside. "Each time I come, the warm moist air and the flowery scents of the oils never fail to remind me of my childhood."

The first room they entered was dimly lit, with blood-red walls bearing the imprint of blue palms: charms against the evil eye, Zoé explained. Women in traditional dress moved languorously through the room, exuding a heady aroma reminiscent of strong incense. Claire, who had only known North American health clubs with their pristine interiors dedicated to strenuous exertion, found the thick, languid atmosphere of the *hammam* overwhelming. She stayed close to Zoé, who made her way confidently through a procession of rooms, greeting and being greeted by robed attendants.

At last they reached an oblong central room where a tiny attendant, whose smile revealed gums adorned with blue tattoos, handed them robes and towels and showed them where to leave their clothes. "The moment of truth," Claire said, trying to make light of the awkwardness she was feeling.

"What are you worried about? You look great," Zoé responded, giving her an appraising look which made Claire blush. "I'm the one with the stretch marks and the flaccid stomach, thanks to two pregnancies. See?" she moaned grabbing her flesh. "This is where my waistline used to be."

Zoé's penchant for dramatics made Claire laugh. If anything, Zoé's small, naked body with its surprisingly large breasts was far more voluptuous than her clothes indicated.

After they had undressed, the attendant, who proved to have powerful hands despite her small size, rubbed their bodies with scented oils. Then, wrapped in towels, their feet encased in wooden clogs, they were installed in an open cubicle, alongside other cubicles forming a circle around a pool at the center of the room. A large dome in the ceiling admitted a scant beam of light through a few glazed apertures. The room was filled with a fog of steam and it took several minutes before Claire began to discern the occupants of the other cubicles.

"Isn't it a wonderful scene?" Zoé asked. "It always reminds me of Delacroix's lush paintings of Morocco." Claire agreed and wished she had a camera with her, although she doubted she would be allowed to use it. As far as she could tell, she and Zoé were the only foreigners in the room.

"It's strange," Zoé was saying as she reclined on the cushions spread out on the marble platform. "I've had no desire to return to Oran. The privileged colonial life we led there was wonderful in many ways, but I couldn't wait to get away. And I did, as soon as I could persuade my parents to allow me to study in France. When they followed, I had no reason to return. I have no patience with the nostalgia expressed by my old friends for the lost charms of their privileged upbringing. And yet I was delighted to find this place. Somehow, when I come here, I rediscover the texture of my childhood. An enclosing, comforting world, inhabited exclusively by females."

"I've been looking for a way to return to the past as

well," Claire said, thinking how easily confidences were shared in the steamy shadows of this room.

"It's age, my dear," Zoé said, rearranging the towel wrapped around her head so that only her small, childlike face peered out from the voluminous turban. "Until thirty, you spend your time running away from your childhood, trying to pass for a grown-up. Once the world starts treating you like an adult, you spend the rest of your life trying to figure out how it is you turned out as you did."

Claire found herself disoriented by her misty surroundings, but the effect was not unpleasant. She felt light-headed and removed from herself, as if her body in its nakedness belonged to the room, alongside the other round, turban-wrapped forms about her. Her voice sounded unusually languorous to her own ears. "You're right. I have a feeling the past is finally catching up with me in all kinds of ways. Those panic episodes didn't just appear out of the blue."

"Sometimes, they do," Zoé said without shifting her position. "It could be physiological, but I suppose that's been ruled out. Anything specific come to mind?"

"Not really, but there's plenty to choose from. Even as a child, I felt there was something odd about my family. I was the only one in my circle of friends with a mother who took off on mysterious trips into the countryside and spent her days behind closed doors struggling with blocks of wood. I used to lie about her to my friends to make her seem more like a regular Mom. Suddenly everything changed. No more trips, no more art, only a persistent sadness. I never understood what happened to her and I tried not to think about it. Now, it seems I can hardly think of anything else. Marta's been no help, but her evasiveness convinces me I'm on to something. It's all tied to the time she left me to come to Paris."

"Interesting that you say she *left* you," Zoé said sitting up, roused by the possibility she had stumbled on to something significant. "You were about twelve then, weren't you? Old enough to understand time, and yet you saw her absence as some kind of abandonment."

"You're right," Claire agreed. "I'm not even sure how long she was away. I didn't miss her actively, but there was always the fear, barely acknowledged, that I would never see her again. In a way, my apprehensions proved correct. The person who went away did not return."

"Perhaps on some level you wanted her to stay away. All children wish their parents dead at one time or another. Of course, when something happens to fulfill their wish, the guilt can be very painful."

Now it was Claire's turn to sit up. "You think I'm looking for an explanation so that I can displace my guilt? If something else, something external, was responsible for her transformation then I'm off the hook. Is that what you think?"

"Take it easy, Claire. I'm not accusing you of anything. It sounds to me as if your mother suffered a classic depression. There may not be any mystery behind it, you know. The most unlikely people find themselves suddenly, for no apparent reason, sad and weary of life. Depression is hard to understand even when the person concerned sits across from you week after week and you use all the skills at your command to find the source of the pain. Take my advice, leave it alone."

Claire stared at Zoé in disbelief. Why was everyone attempting to dissuade her from her search? "It's one thing for Adrian or Marta to tell me to forget it, but you're an analyst."

"Yes, and you're my friend. I don't want to see you make yourself unhappy."

Claire felt too weary to press her point any further and they lay in silence for several minutes on their hard marble couches. She had been reading about Rousseau's paranoia and wondered if it were catching. Or maybe it was Lucinda's influence; Lucinda insisted everything in life happened for a reason, refusing to acknowledge the crazy, haphazard way events unfolded. Claire was grateful when Zoé suggested they try the pool to cool themselves off. After the initial shock, she felt freshly alert. Apparently, so did Zoé, ready to resume their conversation. "I'm sorry I upset you. I'm afraid I have little patience at the moment with people who cling to the past. I have Simon to thank for that."

Her bitter tone worried Claire and made her feel guilty. She had intended to find out what was troubling Zoé and instead she had prattled on about herself, making her friend feel even worse. "No, I'm the one who's sorry. Forgive me for being so stupidly self-absorbed. You sound miserable," she said reaching for her friend's cold, wet hand. "Please tell me what's wrong."

"I am upset and I've been dying to tell you about it, but not on the telephone. Well, here goes," she said, taking a deep breath.

"For years Simon has talked about a special teacher he had when he was thirteen. A young woman, fresh out of school and only a few years older than her students, who changed the course of his life. He ascribed all the virtues in the world to her. She was the one who recognized his abilities and set him on the road that eventually permitted him to attend one of the top schools in the country. Before they parted, she introduced him to Stendhal, lent him books, and arranged for him to take part in a competitive examination that served as a springboard for his escape from the working-class suburb of Lille where he was born. He confessed to me that he trembled with excitement whenever he was near her. When he left the region, he lost track of her.

"About a year ago, he began to talk about finding her. I suspect it had something to do with his manuscript on Stendhal being rejected. Perhaps he wanted to return to the person who had opened up the world to him and given him the confidence to believe in himself. Perhaps he was searching for someone who would be more sympathetic and understanding than his wife. I must admit I'm not as attentive to Simon's complaints as I ought to be. I'll spare you the tedious details of how he managed to track her down. All I can say is that he was entirely obsessed with the project. It became the focus of his existence. In the end he found her, living near the town where they first met."

Zoé's story roused Claire even more than the cold immersion. "How incredible. Well, go on. What happened next?"

"It is an extraordinary story, but I must confess I was annoyed with Simon — and jealous. This woman had assumed such an important role in his life, I kept wishing he would find her an put and end to his fantasy. After all, she had to be in her fifties by now. How much resemblance could she bear to the nineteen-year-old teacher Simon had known?

"Simon never did tell me when he found her. I suppose the event was too important to expose to my critical scrutiny. That came later when she showed up at our door. But I'm getting ahead of myself. Anyway, it seems he wrote to her and received a friendly reply. She did not, however, grant his request for a meeting, saying she wanted him to remember her as she had been. A little strange, don't you think? I mean that's the sort of thing a woman might say to a former lover, not a student.

"Simon would not give up. The next time he was in the region visiting his mother, he decided to force a meeting. As luck would have it, she answered the door. Simon swears he recognized her at once, and she, flattered by his reaction, relented and invited him in. They talked all afternoon. She told him she had been married, had a daughter, and was now divorced. God only knows what version Simon gave of his own life. He did tell her about his manuscript on Stendhal and she expressed a desire to read it. As they parted, she volunteered that she came to Paris occasionally for a little cultural diversion. Simon gave her his card and invited her to call him. He left her house in a state of great excitement. The meeting he had longed for had finally taken place and his illusions remained intact. She was still the charming, cultivated woman he had adored. Our desire to make reality conform to our longings is a very powerful force, you see. In Simon's case, one meeting did not suffice to undo the fantasy he had elaborated over the years."

The arrival of two attendants interrupted Zoé's tale. "It's time for our massage," she said. Claire was dying to hear the rest of the story, but for the next hour her attention was taken over by painful and pleasurable sensations wrung from her body by the deft hands of her tiny masseuse. Every joint in her body, including the vertebrae in her back, was made to crack. Her limbs were twisted with such apparent violence, she was amazed to have them fall back into place undamaged. Her flesh, kneaded persistently, turned to putty, incapable of ever tensing again. Even the soles of her feet were scraped and massaged into a state of total acquiescence. Then her body was lathered with some abrasive substance, rinsed off, enveloped in towels, and left to repose in semi-darkness. Claire doubted she would ever rouse herself enough to get dressed. But when the attendant returned with their clothes a short while later, she felt rested, as if she had slept for hours. She could see why Zoé was attached to this place.

Zoé resumed her story in an Arab café next door to the *Hammam* where they stopped for some mint tea. "It's a pretty sad tale from here on in, I'm afraid," she said, stirring her tea. "I don't know how many times Simon actually saw his teacher before the change set in, but the inevitable happened. Simon grew bored and began to invent excuses for not being able to meet her when she called. She became more insistent, unwilling to recognize the sad truth that Simon preferred his fantasy of her to actually spending afternoons with an aging, retired schoolteacher. One day, he simply forgot he had arranged to meet her and she came to the house looking for him. I must say I felt sorry for her and I was furious with Simon for having created an embarrassing situation."

"What did you do?"

"I invited her in. I suspect she was curious to see her rival. The poor woman didn't realize I was no threat to her. Her true rival was her own younger self, enshrined eternally in Simon's memory. Simon still sees her from time to time out of a reluctant sense of duty, as if she were some elderly relative from the provinces he feels obliged to entertain. The whole episode has become an embarrassment. He would kill me if he knew I'd told you. Please don't say a word about it to Adrian. Although after the stupid way he's behaved, I don't know why I should care about his feelings."

"I promise I won't say anything. Still, Simon's obsession sounds pretty harmless," Claire said, wondering about Zoé's anger.

"Do you think so? Simon's actions came as a very painful surprise. I would be less upset if Simon had taken up with a real mistress. As it is, I catch myself looking at him as if he were a stranger. You believe you know someone and then he goes ahead and does something so out of character, you can't think of him in the same way ever again. Your curiosity about your mother could have a similarly unpleasant ending. If you find out some awful truth about her, you may end up with all your assumptions destroyed. Not a happy prospect, believe me, Claire."

Zoé was on the verge of tears. Claire restrained her impulse to hug Zoé and cry with her. She had to do better than that. Somehow, she had to help Zoé see Simon's behavior in a less hopeless light.

"You know I like Simon," she began, choosing her words with care, "but I'm not about to defend him. It's you I care about right now and I can see how much he's upset you. Still, isn't it possible you're exaggerating the gravity of his offense just a little?"

They left the café and Claire linked her arm through Zoé's, wanting to retain the physical intimacy they had shared in the baths. "You're always telling me how monotonous you find your life. And here's Simon, who's done something so out of the ordinary, it makes you look at him with amazement. He's let you know there's more to him than you assumed. Who knows what else lies hidden behind that bland civil servant exterior? Surely you don't want to live with someone whose actions are always predictable. Now that would be *really* monotonous."

Zoé responded with a wan smile. "You may be right. Perhaps I am overreacting. My responses are not what they should be these days. This morning I was furious with a taxi driver because he failed to follow the route I suggested to him. I seem to have lost my emotional compass. Being with you makes me feel a little saner. Thanks for putting up with me."

"Hey, what are friends for?"

Walking home after they had parted, Claire worried about Zoé. She doubted her words would change Zoé's view of Simon. She tried to picture Zoé and Simon together, as she used to do when she envied their happy marriage — easy dancing partners bringing out each other's best moves — but all she could see were two people avoiding each other. Simon certainly wasn't easy to be with these days, and yet, much as she sympathized with Zoé, she understood Simon's mad pursuit of an old dream.

No wonder he had turned to the past for solace. Certainly there was none to be found near Zoé these days. But then she was not married to Simon. Who knew what went on between people who have listened to each other's complaints for as long as Zoé and Simon had? Perhaps a kind of self-protectiveness takes over if you're to survive the long haul. The strange bargains struck by couples to allow their marriages to continue seemed strange only to outsiders. She and Adrian had been together only three years, and she could already see certain spots where the fabric of their marriage was wearing thin, and patterns of avoidance had become necessary to protect those areas.

She thought of Rousseau, whose relations with women had been so exalted in the pages of his novels and so troubled in life. Even the mute, obedient Thérèse, his mistress, had grown stronger and bolder as he neared the end. According to what Claire had been reading, Thérèse had found her tongue with the passing years and it often turned sharply against the old man. After his death, she took up with a servant in the household of the Marquis de Girardin, and came into her own. In this second, more equal union, she was the one with the upper hand. As guardian of the Rousseau legend, pursued by scholars who paid her obsequious attention in order to win her favor, she found her own kind of glory while retaining her usual sense of modesty. "What!" she exclaimed with unconscious irony in a rare, preserved letter, "Because Rousseau did a poor girl who did not know how to read or write the honor of having her wash his linen and cook his soup and at times share his bed — must this poor girl be turned into a heroine?"

The question echoed across centuries as Claire contemplated the peculiarities of the marriage compact. The sad glimpse she had just had into her friends' marriage made her long for Adrian. She climbed the stairs to Marta's apartment — the old elevator once again not working — hoping to find him home. She needed the reassurance of his presence, needed to see the way his face responded when he caught sight of her. Surely she could overcome his resistance when she told him of the physical bond now uniting them. For all his preoccupation, she knew she could count on Adrian if she expressed her need for him in strong enough terms. He had to be reminded that he missed her as well. Left to his own devices, Adrian forgot about himself and everyone near him. She decided to heed Marta's advice and find a way to lure him away from his work.

SEVENTEEN

Adrian did not require much persuasion to set his work aside for the evening. In fact, he seemed eager to be rescued from it. During their long pleasant dinner in a restaurant near the Palais-Royal she said nothing to him about the baby, not wanting to dispel the easy, affectionate tone of their exchanges. Walking back to Marta's apartment, with Adrian's arm lightly around her waist, she still hesitated. The moment was too good, too precious to threaten with conflict.

How rare such evenings had become, she thought with regret. When they first lived together, she had teased him about wanting to keep her a prisoner since he never wanted to share their time together with others. Although she had sometimes protested, she loved every minute of those intense months when watching Adrian perform the most insignificant task had filled her with acute pleasure. Of course, it couldn't last; life would have become claustrophobic if it had, but she had hoped to recapture some small measure of that early excitement during their stay in Paris. Instead, thanks to Marcel, they were almost never alone.

She was always surprised to see how easily they recovered their strong attachment, given half a chance, like tonight. It was as if the banal phrases they exchanged rushing past each other everyday — Has the mail arrived? Do you need anything dropped off at the cleaners? When will you be home? —were, in fact, in code, concealing one essential message: I have no time for you right now, but I remember how it feels to be oblivious to everything but you.

One of the things she liked best about marriage, she decided, was the surprise of falling in love again, without the fear and uncertainty that accompanied the initial, tentative coming-together of strangers. She had grown used to the role that had become her lot in marriage: the guardian of the seal of intimacy — the person who every now and then could make Adrian stop his work, who initiated the necessary air-clearing conversations and created a certain measure of turbulence to stir the emotions. Adrian, in his own way, appreciated this division of labor, demonstrating his gratitude in all the little ways he tried to please her. Adrian was not a man who stinted on affection as long as Claire provided the right circumstances: he was like a person who enjoyed swimming, but who only remembered that pleasure when someone brought him to the seashore.

Crossing the courtyard and gardens of the ancient royal Palace, they walked beneath the arches of the double colonnade enclosing shuttered antique shops and art galleries. The place was still, deserted, a sheltered island of fading regal perfection, turning its back on the noise and bustle of neighboring streets. Claire put her arm through Adrian's and, trusting the good feeling between them, said, "I have something to tell you."

"I know," he said squeezing her arm. "It seems as if we haven't talked in ages. You haven't told me how you're getting on with the countess. Have you been feeling all right? Any sign of those panic symptoms?"

"I'm fine. The work is going well, but that's not what I want to talk about. There's something important I need to tell you."

"Hold on a minute," he said suddenly. "How magnificent the square looks at this hour. It's easy to imagine the ghosts of the past in such a setting, isn't it? You know, this space was once one of the most popular playgrounds in Europe. Magicians, acrobats, sword swallowers performed here. At night, it became a market for swift, coarse, dangerous pleasures, as one historian described it. Can't you just see it?"

Claire was familiar with the way Adrian abruptly interrupted conversations to comment on some detail that caught his eye, or to express a thought provoked by the passing scene. When she had first objected to this annoying habit, Adrian had responded with astonishment: Didn't she understand that if he waited until the conversation ended, they would have left behind whatever it was he wanted her to notice? Of course he was listening, but that didn't make him blind, did it? She had trained herself to tolerate his interjections. She said nothing now, knowing that as soon as she spoke she would have his entire attention. For a moment, however, she enjoyed the prospect of shaking his composure.

As soon as they left the square, Adrian's attention returned to the conversation he had interrupted. She had to give him credit for that. "You had something to tell me," he said, his arm once again holding her against him. "What was it?"

Claire stopped and turned to face him. How relaxed and unsuspecting he looked, his eyes expressing only affection. She felt like an executioner about to deliver a fatal blow, but she chased the thought away, remembering who needed her protection most. "We're going to have a baby," she said, trying to keep her voice steady.

The look of bewilderment on his face was almost comical. "What are you talking about?"

"I'm pregnant."

"But how can that be? How did this happen?"

"You know I went off the pill. A diaphragm simply isn't as reliable. We just proved that."

"I thought you were being so careful."

Claire did not like the accusatory note in his voice. "I didn't plan it, if that's what you're thinking. It came as a surprise to me as well."

He seemed at a loss for words and simply stared at her with a stricken expression. She almost felt sorry for him. But when he spoke, her sympathy was displaced by anger.

"It's not too late for an abortion, is it?" he asked when they resumed walking.

So this was his first response. Despite his previous objections, she had expected more from him. Angry tears rose in her eyes and she struggled to keep them back. "No, it's not too late, but abortion is not an option." She was surprised how cool and steady her voice sounded.

"You're not seriously thinking of going through with this pregnancy? We talked about not having children. You agreed."

"It was your decision. You decided. I went along with it because your feelings were stronger than mine at the time. In any case, everything has changed now."

"Have you thought this through? Do you realize what you're taking on? What about all the traveling you do for your work? You have no idea how a child restricts your life."

"Other people manage, why can't we? In any case, I'm tired of being at the beck and call of anyone who contacts Lucinda. I'm tired of Lucinda telling me how wonderful some commission I don't want to do will be for my career. I'm tired of having a career. I want to concentrate on my own ideas for a change. The panic attacks made me reconsider my approach to my work even before I knew I was pregnant."

"As I said, you haven't thought this through. For one thing, you could not go near your darkroom if you persist in this crazy idea. Have you thought of what the chemicals you use would do to a fetus?"

Claire was at a loss for a moment. She had not considered the darkroom.

Sensing his advantage, Adrian's tone softened. "Come on Claire," he said, pulling her towards him. "We've been so happy together. Why spoil it?"

She moved out of his embrace, feeling they had never been further apart. "I would not be happy if I did what you ask." She found it hard to remember they had ever been happy. Did she really want to have a child with this unfeeling man?

Oblivious of her mood, he put his hand on her back and gently caressed her neck. "I don't want to lose what we have. The passion, the freedom, the spontaneity. I know what a child will do to all that. It will turn our world upside down. I love Melissa, but I can't see myself raising an infant or running after a toddler. We don't have to decide anything now, but please think about what I'm saying."

She found Adrian's soothing tone far more annoying than his earlier confusion. She felt him gaining strength as her own position weakened. " I suggest you think about it as well," she said. "If you can't see yourself becoming a father again, I may have to do this alone. That wouldn't be very good for our closeness either, would it?"

Adrian seemed to recoil from her new ferocity. She was glad she could sound more convinced than she felt.

"All right," he said finally, his voice careful, neutral. "I will think about it. We'll both give it some thought."

They were now close to Marta's apartment. The fog had grown thicker, shrouding their way and dimming the lights around them. It dampened the antagonism that had flared up only moments ago. A temporary truce of sorts prevailed. When Adrian took her arm to guide her through the darkness, she did not pull away.

She was disappointed to find Marta still awake when they entered the flat. She was in no mood for further conversation.

"You just missed Antoine," Marta said, referring to her grandson. "That boy has no sense of time. He sleeps all day and roams the streets at night. He came to ask for money. I have a feeling he's in some kind of trouble. Of course there's no point in talking to Louise or her husband, they would only be angry I gave him anything. But what am I to do? I can't simply wash my hands of him the way his parents seem to have done. I don't know how I'll ever get to sleep, but don't let me keep you up. You must be tired."

Adrian gave Claire a meaningful look as if to say, you see the trouble children bring, and went off to the bedroom. Claire tried to distract Marta from her worries by drawing her attention to the luxuriant bouquet of roses that graced the living room mantelpiece. They hadn't been there when Claire left for dinner.

"They are lovely, aren't they?" Marta said, a smile momentarily softening her worried expression. "Henri brought them. I'll tell you something, my child. If you want a man to bring you flowers, you must take a lover, not a husband."

Claire's weariness at the moment made her feel older than Marta, the eternal *femme fatale*. Zoé was right when she insisted they were no match for women of Marta's generation. "I'll try to remember your advice. Now I must go to bed. I'm exhausted."

"Well, if you must," Marta said, looking disappointed. "Thank God for Gertrude. She appreciates distraction at any hour."

EIGHTEEN

The next few days were so unusually eventful, Claire and Adrian found it easy to avoid further discussion. Both were wary of stumbling into the breach created by the harsh words they had exchanged. It frightened them to see how quickly they had moved from certainty about each other to this new hesitant phase where they hardly dared to speak. They retreated to the safety of silence, watching each other for some sign of softening that would signal a change of heart.

News of their friends' problems proved a welcome distraction. It was much easier to talk about their friends than about themselves.

Claire was shocked to hear that lovely, young Sophie, who carried herself as if some invisible crown entitled her to the best in life, had chosen to move in with Marcel. What did she see in her former professor? Claire wondered. And how did she manage to fit herself into his cramped apartment where no one was ever invited to visit? Marcel must have displaced his precious books to make room for Sophie — an extraordinary declaration, she thought.

Adrian's anger when he reported the news startled her. "It's not all that unusual for a professor to take up with one of his students," she said, trying to calm him. "In France people are more tolerant of such liaisons."

"Well, this is a turnabout. You defending Marcel. I can't believe Sophie's parents will be as understanding as you suggest. He's more than twice her age, and he has abused their friendship as well as his position as her teacher. Do you realize Sophie is only a few years older than Melissa? No wonder he's been avoiding me."

Claire understood that the sense of betrayal Adrian expressed had more to do with his work than with Melissa.

His discussions with Marcel on the progress of his research had become a necessary habit. Marcel's absence and her own jarring news were bound to disrupt the pursuit of his work. She felt a little sorry for him, but she did not allow her heart to soften towards him. The decision that faced her required detachment.

Adrian's prediction about Sophie's parents proved to be correct. When they could not persuade their daughter to leave Marcel, Gilbert and Anne-Marie consulted Zoé, who specialized in the problems of adolescents and young adults. Zoé calmed them and advised patience. To Claire she confessed that the coupling of Sophie with Marcel disturbed her. "My God, if Juliette ever does anything this stupid, I think I will forget all my training and forcibly drag her home."

While talk of their scandalous behavior swirled around them, the offending pair dropped out of sight. Now that the university term was over, they could have gone anywhere. Adrian made no attempt to find Marcel, and Marcel, wherever he was, remained silent.

During this time, Marta became increasingly troubled about her grandson. Antoine, after borrowing money from his grandmother, had vanished. According to Marta, his parents were not particularly anxious about his whereabouts, insisting that he often disappeared for days, only to resurface when he was hungry or needed a shower. Marta was scandalized by their indifference and Claire heard her lecturing her daughter about parental responsibility. Marta, however, did not tell Louise about the money she had given Antoine; she had often been reprimanded by Antoine's parents for encouraging his idleness.

Claire felt as if all the anguish she was witnessing between parents and children was intended as a warning. She tried to reassure Marta as best she could. From the little she had seen of Antoine, it seemed to her he could well take care of himself.

A week after his departure, Marta received a postcard from Antoine telling her not to worry. He was in Amsterdam living with friends, and might remain there indefinitely.

Marta's worries took a new form. Amsterdam was the drug capital of Europe and Antoine had surely not chosen that city at random. She feared the worst and insisted he had to be brought back before he became truly lost. She summoned her son-in-law (with whom she had an easier relationship than with her daughter) urging him to go after Antoine. Her son-in-law listened with a great deal of sympathy. He liked Marta and wished that Louise had more of her mother's spirit — Louise's silent stubbornness made it impossible to discuss Antoine's problems. Nevertheless, he rejected Marta's plan. It might be a good thing for everyone, he explained, if Antoine stayed away for a while. His presence had become a strain on the entire family, and as for drugs, they were available in Paris as well as in Amsterdam. No, he really couldn't see the benefit of pursuing Antoine.

Marta wept after her son-in-law left and decided to set off alone to find Antoine, even though his postcard had not provided her with an address. Claire, Adrian, and the ever-faithful Henri tried to dissuade her from going, suggesting she wait at least until she heard from Antoine again. Claire enlisted Zoé's help. Zoé came over and told Marta that, to the best of her professional knowledge, Antoine could only be helped by his own resolve. A defiant Louise also appeared, accusing Marta of alienating Antoine from his parents by excessively indulging him; Marta's decision to follow him to Amsterdam, she insisted, was a veiled attempt to demonstrate what an inadequate mother she, Louise, had turned out to be.

Marta heard them all, even Louise, with an unusual degree of calm, and then went on with her preparations. She spent hours on the telephone talking to crisis centers about how to deal with runaways and drug users. She amassed lists of suggestions and names of people to contact in Amsterdam. In odd moments away from her investigation, she wept, telling Claire her heart ached whenever she thought that Antoine had become such a nuisance to his family, they were prepared to write him off. Antoine, she argued, needed to know someone cared enough about him to do something desperate to help him. Too many people, she felt, failed to intervene in the lives of others, and she was not going to make that mistake with her grandson. "We have clothed selfishness and indifference in the guise of politeness and pretend we are respecting one another's privacy when we are simply avoiding inconvenient involvement," she said, packing her bags. She left, promising Henri and Claire that she would call frequently.

Claire sided with Marta. She admired the older woman's willingness to fight for her grandson when everyone else was prepared to let him drift. If anyone could help the troubled boy, Marta was the person to do it.

When the telephone rang the day after Marta's departure, Claire hoped it was her godmother with good news. But the call was from Gertrude. After inquiring about Marta, she asked Claire to come and see her. Claire was reluctant, but agreed, feeling that by taking Marta's place she was doing something to help her friend. She assumed that Gertrude, confined to her apartment by her husband's illness, missed Marta's visits.

She found Gertrude noticeably calmer than she had been during her previous visit. Jacques was away, Gertrude explained. Twice a week, a community van drove him to a recreation center for Alzheimer patients, providing her with some badly needed respite. "He's as happy as a child every time the van comes to pick him up," she said. "If they didn't bring him back, he would never miss his home. Any day now, I expect him to return from one of these outings and look at me without a sign of recognition."

Gertrude fell silent after these remarks, busying herself with the tea tray. Her movements, precise and ceremonious, reflected the almost sterile order of the apartment. Had everything extraneous been removed for Jacques' benefit?

Claire felt she was being an inadequate stand-in for Marta. She tried to ease the awkward silence with some half-remembered comments on Jacques' disease offered by a neurologist whose photo she had taken for a magazine story. She had become skillful at putting her subjects at ease by encouraging them to talk about themselves while she concentrated on her equipment and the effect she wanted to achieve. It was obvious that Gertrude was now responding to her in a similar automatic fashion. Clearly, her mind was elsewhere.

Claire didn't know Gertrude well enough to understand what this preoccupation meant. She had run out of things to say and began to wonder how soon she could leave. Gertrude, seeing her reach for her shoulder bag, emerged from her distracted state, anxious to retain her. "Forgive me for being such poor company," she said, turning to Claire with a faint, pinched smile. "Let's not talk about Jacques and his awful illness for a moment. I've asked you to come for a reason. Only I'm having trouble finding the right words. It's not easy to tell you what I have to say. It concerns your mother and Marta," She was now looking directly at Claire.

Claire found herself turning towards the closed window, unable to meet Gertrude's eyes. For the first time since her arrival in France, a sudden rush of panic threatened to overwhelm her. She felt her heart pounding, her head throbbing, and she was finding it difficult to breathe. She had a strong desire to rush out of the room away from Gertrude's voice. Now that she was close to learning the truth about her mother — she was certain that Gertrude was about to reveal something important — she no longer knew if she wanted to hear it. All the techniques she had practiced so patiently seemed beyond her at this moment, but she managed to stay in the room. Her only concession to her overreactive body was to ask Gertrude if she could open the window.

When they were seated across from each other again, Gertrude went on. "Marta has told me how troubled she is by the questions you continue to ask about your mother. Don't be offended; we're old friends. I can understand her reticence. It was a painful time for her. I knew all about it because Marta has always confided in me. I think I'm probably the only person other than Marta who knows what happened. The others are dead. I've told her I believe you're entitled to the truth. Since Marta can't or won't talk about it I feel I must. It seems to me the dead have no right to take their secrets with them when these secrets lead to painful unanswered questions. I hope Marta will forgive me."

How strange it was, Claire thought, that in her obsessive search she had never considered Gertrude. And what an unlikely source she seemed. Claire could not imagine Marta confiding in this sad, distant woman. Did she regret her trust in Gertrude, and was that the reason she continually warned Claire not to share confidences with Zoé? Gertrude's low, neutral voice helped to calm Claire. "I want to know everything you can tell me," she said, trying to match Gertrude's tone. "Please go on."

Gertrude nodded, smoothing back her short gray hair, and leaned forward. "There's no gentle way to say this. Your mother and Marta's husband, Bruno, were lovers. There was something about Bruno's political zeal that drew women to him. His dedication made him seem larger than life, although he was rather a small man and not very robust. I don't think Bruno and Dolly meant to fall in love, but they did. It was a *coup de foudre*, a bolt of lightning. They could have no more prevented it than poor Jacques can keep from cleaning the courtyard."

"Did it go on for a long time?" Claire asked, finding her voice again.

"The affair began when Marta was away at a congress for translators in Zurich. They intended to end it as soon as she returned, but it didn't work out that way. The liaison continued, but discreetly. It couldn't have been easy for Bruno or Dolly to lie to Marta, they were not people practiced in deception, but they did it to protect her. They had agreed the affair would never lead to anything. They believed they could keep it from Marta until Dolly's departure and then she would never know.

"These kinds of situations rarely end well. Sooner or later, the web of concealment we weave so diligently snags in some unexpected fashion and unravels. In Bruno and Dolly's case, the fragile thread was the obvious one. It has undone women since the beginning of time. She found herself pregnant. She told no one, not even Bruno, and arranged to have an abortion. It's probably hard for someone your age to imagine the desperate measures women resorted to in the not-so-distant past in order to obtain an abortion. It was particularly difficult for Dolly, finding herself in a strange city and unwilling to seek help from the people she knew. Inevitably, there were complications, and she began hemorrhaging shortly after she returned to her studio. She probably would have died if Marta, concerned by her inability to reach Dolly, had not come around. She had to persuade the *concièrge* to let her into the flat where she found Dolly bleeding and nearly unconscious."

Claire heard an involuntary moan escape through her lips and her arms crossed in front of her, cradling her middle, as if she were protecting her body from a blow. Gertrude looked at her curiously, but went on with her story.

"While Dolly convalesced in the hospital, Bruno told Marta what had happened. Eventually, they managed to patch things up. They were all three reasonable people and the feelings of affection they had for one another proved stronger than guilt or betrayal. But I don't think any of them ever recovered from the near tragedy. When I heard the questions you were asking Marta, I realized Dolly had brought her misery home. Because children tend to blame themselves for their parents' unhappiness, I felt you had a right to know." Gertrude paused for a moment, waiting for Claire to agree. Claire nodded, not trusting her voice. "Marta should have been the one to tell you. Her silence forces me to speak," Gertrude added, as if she were justifying herself to the absent Marta.

Eventually, Claire would question the reasons Gertrude gave for revealing Dolly's secret. But on the day of their meeting she was too stunned by what she had learned to think of anything else. It was raining heavily when she left Gertrude's apartment, but she decided to walk. Her head was spinning and she hoped the exercise would calm her. Gertrude's words had provided a key to the past and now even her fondest memories shimmered with newly revealed meaning.

She felt no sorrow for Dolly as yet. Perhaps that would come. Anger was more within her reach just now. She thought of the child she had been, of the quiet, pleasant home she had taken for granted and the puzzling changes that followed her mother's return from Paris. How could Dolly have been so reckless with the happiness they had once shared? How could she have risked it all — her family, her friendship with Marta, her work — for a brief episode of passion doomed from the beginning? And what were Marta's feelings towards her, Claire, the daughter of the friend who had betrayed her? She had found Dolly's trail, but it seemed to lead only to painful considerations.

Was Dolly's story a cautionary tale, a warning to her daughter from beyond the grave? Claire didn't want her mother's sadness to influence her decision. She already felt a growing sense of certainty about the child. She hadn't considered the practical objections Adrian had raised and they didn't seem to matter. She concentrated instead on the

167

feeling inside her, the flicker of desire for the unborn child, watching it wax and wane until its steady flame seemed unquenchable. Even now, walking in the rain, her thoughts in turmoil, she felt it glowing steadily.

She was exhausted and no closer to forgiving her mother when she headed home. Adrian was waiting for her. "My God, Claire, do you realize what time it is? Where have you been? I was beginning to worry."

Claire noted his concern and it comforted her. Despite their bitter words, he still cared for her. "I'm sorry," she said, starting to cry.

"It's all right." He drew her close to him, gently caressing her hair. "What's wrong?" he asked, "you look so tired." His tenderness broke down the fragile control she had maintained since leaving Gertrude and unleashed more tears. She was grateful Adrian didn't press for an explanation. She couldn't talk about Dolly just yet, but she held on to him fiercely, needing his comfort. It felt good to be back in his arms. He loves me, he will come around, she repeated to herself until she grew calmer.

"Feeling better?" he asked after a while. She nodded. "Good," he said, "I have wonderful news. Marta called while you were out. She's found Antoine. They're coming home."

NINETEEN

Marta returned from Amsterdam weary but triumphant. "I am a little tired," she admitted to Claire, who expressed concern at the change in Marta's appearance. "I caught something in Amsterdam I can't seem to shake." The restless manner and the swift, darting gestures that usually animated her movements and belied her age were gone. Marta suddenly looked old and frail, a shuffling old woman with puffed, teary eyes who took to her bed with a sigh of relief.

Claire felt alarmed by Marta's weakened state. Her own concerns had to be set aside temporarily. It would be indecent to saddle Marta in her present condition with her urgent need to talk — she had not yet said anything to anyone about what she had learned from Gertrude, needing Marta's confirmation before she could speak — and so Claire kept her silence while Marta recuperated.

During her wakeful moments, Marta described how she had found Antoine. "At first I despaired. There are so many young drifters in Amsterdam; they're indistinguishable, no matter where they come from. You can certainly see the new Europe there. These young people have no country but their own society. Even the ones who come from lands bitterly divided by ethnic strife seem to have left the old hatreds behind like a bad dream. They appear to live in a world of their own, linked by music, drugs, and a deep suspicion of all ideologies, disdaining anything they were taught at home."

"As I wandered among these young people looking for Antoine, I was reminded of the desperate weeks I spent trying to track down Bruno when he had been arrested following a bloody demonstration against the French occupation of Algeria. I was afraid they were going to deport

169

him and I had to find him before that happened. This was not his first arrest and the struggle had turned fierce, as it did in America during the Vietnam War. I was racing against time with our future at stake. I remember running for days on end, from one *préfecture* to the next, borrowing money where I could to bribe my way to him. Of course, I was much younger then. In Amsterdam, thank God, it took only two days to locate Antoine. I walked into a shelter for homeless youths and there he was, a shabby lost child. I can't tell you what it did to me to see him there in those awful conditions."

"What was his reaction? He must have been shocked to see you."

"He was, and relieved as well. He confessed everything. His arrangement with his so-called friends hadn't lasted more than a few days. Since then he had been hungry, alone, and too ashamed to come home. He admitted he has been 'fooling around with drugs' for years. Nothing 'serious,' he assured me, but he agreed he needed help. He's already been in a treatment center once, but he didn't last long. No wonder Louise and her husband are fed up. I wish they hadn't kept things from me; we could have avoided a great many quarrels. This time, I believe Antoine is serious. The shock of seeing his grandmother pursuing him across Europe must have done something to him. As soon as I get my strength back, I'm going to ask your friend Zoé to help me find a good facility for him. I feel very optimistic about Antoine. After all, he must have inherited *something* of Bruno's strength."

Claire thought for a moment about that familial relationship. What would Bruno Berkmann, a highly disciplined man committed to a lifelong cause, have made of this grandson, drifting aimlessly through life? Perhaps they would have found something in common. Weren't they both, after all, at odds with society?

"You know, during the time I spent looking for him in

Amsterdam," Marta continued, pursuing a similar line of thought, "I couldn't help thinking how different Antoine's generation is from my own. For one thing, their lives seem so dull, so monotonously restricted by their lack of interest in anything larger than their own existence. God knows, we were mistaken in many of our beliefs, but at least we cared about something. We had passion, conviction, and hope to give our lives meaning. No wonder Antoine and his friends resort to drugs — just to feel something. I can't pretend I like growing old, but I wouldn't want to be young again if it meant being as disconnected from the world as these young people are."

Claire stayed close to Marta's side and waited for the right moment to speak. "You're everything a daughter should be," Marta said to her in appreciation. Claire, who had once wished for these words, felt like a traitor as she looked after Marta. Wasn't her attention an attempt to hasten Marta's recovery so that she could knock her down again by forcing her to relive painful memories? At times, she saw her ministrations as a form of penance for Dolly's betrayal of Marta.

Claire felt that Dolly had betrayed her daughter as well as her friend. Dolly's life in Paris, as Gertrude had revealed it, had no connection to the placid, comfortable world where she and her father had waited for her return. And when she had come back no longer able to work but still, to all appearances, the good wife and mother, her thoughts belonged to a world they knew nothing about. Claire remembered how much she had loved the letters her mother sent home from Paris, continuing in them a custom, established when Claire was a child, of decorating with drawings the margins of the notes they left for each other.

It pained Claire to remember the good things. The letters had been lies, she reminded herself, imaginatively decorated lies, to hide the truth about Dolly's life. Perhaps the lies kept her mother from work as well. Dolly's art had always been highly personal and it might have revealed what she was trying to hide. Had she censored herself to protect her ties to her family? Claire felt her anger wavering. Her perception of Dolly, she realized, was a sort of emotional *trompe l'oeil*: If she thought of her as another woman, an artist, then her heart could not help turning to her in compassion. But once Dolly assumed the features of her mother, then Claire could not forgive her.

Two days after her return, Marta was up and about and acting like her old self. Antoine appeared willing to try anything. He and his parents had talked without anger for the first time in years. Louise, in her conversations with her mother, admitted grudgingly that Marta's efforts may have helped. Marta summoned Zoé to discuss plans for Antoine's treatment. Zoé promised to help find a place for Antoine, preferably some distance from Paris.

When Claire walked Zoé to the Métro, Zoé spoke admiringly of Marta. "That woman is a tower of strength," she said. "I believe she actually made a difference in her grandson's life. I don't know about you, but women like her make me want to lie down and wait for the storm to pass. There's something about her generation, the best among them, that makes me wonder if we could ever measure up. They seem to have been made of tougher matter. Even my own mother, a far more conventional woman, possesses the kind of inner resources in the face of misfortune I don't find in myself. It may seem cruel to say this, but in a way you were lucky to lose your mother when you did. You don't have her shadow hanging over you. From what you've told me, she sounded formidable in her own right."

Claire sidestepped the reference to her mother. "I think the reason we feel inadequate in comparison to Marta's generation," she said, with more evenness than she felt, "is that our lives have been much more sheltered than theirs. It seems paradoxical, doesn't it? Our horizons are far broader because we live in a world where women have been freed of most of the restrictions that formerly bound them. Theoretically, there are no limits to our ambitions. If we fail to live up to the promises we make to ourselves, there are no excuses. We can only blame ourselves. What's been taken away is the struggle and the chance to find out how well we would do against the obstacles these women had to overcome. Not that one wants to go back in time, of course. But the conditions they had to face as women produced the resilience you admire."

"You may be right. I'm feeling terribly inadequate these days. I seem to be letting everything slide and avoiding all conversations that threaten to be contentious. I watch Simon hide his depression behind the evening paper, I see the increasing tension between Simon and Christophe, and Juliette's disapproval directed at all of us, but mostly at me, and I do nothing. I preside over the evening meal, making inane attempts at cheerfulness, hoping we can just get through dinner without some unpleasantness erupting to waylay me before I've had a chance to escape. No, I'm definitely not feeling very competent right now."

Claire knew that Zoé's penchant for self-disparagement belonged to a conversational style, not intended to be taken seriously: something to do with Zoé's oriental childhood where good manners required a show of humility. But the new note of hopelessness she heard in Zoé's voice troubled Claire.

"Things have not improved with Simon, have they?" she asked, giving her friend a hug. "You're letting his problems sap your confidence. I've never seen you so low. So you're not like Marta, or your mother, or any of the female titans your feel you ought to resemble. So what? Neither am I. If you were like them, we couldn't possibly be friends. As it is, I find you sufficiently intimidating. You're a great therapist, a great mother, a splendid hostess and the best friend anyone can ask for. You're also a much better cook than Marta can ever hope to be. Shall I go on?"

"Stop," Zoé said, laughing, "you're making me blush."

They had arrived at the entrance to the Châtelet station when she turned to Claire and asked with mock plaintiveness, "How will I manage without you once you're back in Montréal? Yes, I help a few patients, but you're the only one I can turn to these days. Now that Marta is better, you must promise to put me at the top of your list for the rest of your stay."

On her way back to the flat, Claire ran into Adrian returning from his day at the library. She noticed him before he saw her. He looked tired and preoccupied but when he spotted her his face broke into a big smile. "I have a surprise for you. I think you're going to like it," he said, reaching into his canvas bag. He handed Claire a thick, brown envelope. Inside, she found a catalog of one of Dolly's exhibitions at the Musée des Beaux-Arts in Montréal. The date on it was 1975. "Isn't it wonderful? It's in perfect condition."

"Where did you find it?" Claire asked after a long pause; Adrian's gift had overwhelmed her.

"At a second-hand dealer on St. Michel. I knew you'd want to have it. Come on, let's show it to Marta."

But the dismay they saw on Marta's face when they let themselves into the flat made them forget about Adrian's find. "What's wrong?" Claire asked, thinking of Antoine.

"Gertrude is dead," Marta said, her words uttered with uncharacteristic slowness. "I've just had a call from her son. She threw herself into the Seine sometime last night. They haven't found her body but she left letters explaining what she intended to do. There's one addressed to me. I must go over there, but I can't move."

Claire thought of her meeting with Gertrude. She was certain now that Gertrude had come to her decision before inviting her over. The phrase she had used, "The dead have no right to take their secrets with them," assumed new meaning. Had there been other clues she had missed? She went over the details of their meeting, focusing not on Gertrude's revelations about Dolly, but on Gertrude herself.

She had scarcely known Gertrude, but it seemed doubtful that anyone could have deciphered Gertrude's intentions from her behavior that morning. For the secret she had surrendered, she had kept another, darker one.

Claire looked at Marta sipping a small glass of brandy, and wished she could keep Gertrude's letter from her. She suspected its contents would reveal her conversation with Gertrude. How many more shocks could Marta stand? It was all very well for her and Zoé to speculate about Marta's toughness, but the flesh-and-blood person before her appeared dangerously shaken. She wanted to warn Marta, but how could she do so without upsetting her even more? She remained silent while she fetched the sleeping pill Marta requested and helped her to bed.

Adrian was asleep when she returned to their room. She remembered she had been too surprised to thank him properly for his gift. He had been so pleased to find it; she wished she had responded more generously. Again she noticed how tired he looked and decided to show her appreciation another time. Claire lay beside him, unable to sleep, thinking of the catalog on the chair beside her bed, imagining its journey over the years until Adrian rescued it from some dusty book bin. Adrian's inveterate habit of browsing in second-hand bookstores offered such rewards. Still, she did not understand her own hesitation about touching the pamphlet. With an effort of will she picked it up, turning the pages quietly so as not to disturb Adrian. She was relieved to find that her feelings for Dolly's work had not changed.

TWENTY

Marta did not take to her bed again as Claire had feared. Zoé had been right after all, Marta's spirit was indomitable. After the initial shock, she rallied quickly to lend her support to Gertrude's children.

Gertrude's body was discovered a few kilometers downstream from Paris. An early morning stroller spotted the body entangled in bushes growing near the water's edge and alerted the police. Marta volunteered to help Gertrude's son organize the funeral when he arrived from Montpellier. There were other arrangements to be made for placing Jacques in the institution Gertrude had selected. Marta feared Jacques would decline rapidly in unfamiliar surroundings. Claire remembered what Gertrude had said about how willingly Jacques went along on his outings and how the time was fast approaching when he would be unable to recognize her. She knew these words would have eased Marta's concern, but she couldn't tell her. This was not the time to reveal her meeting with Gertrude. If Marta had learned about it from Gertrude's letter, she said nothing.

Claire was surprised at the large crowd gathered at Père Lachaise Cemetery for Gertrude's funeral. Marta explained that Gertrude and Jacques had been active in various left-wing political organizations most of their lives and Jacques had been well known as a skilled organizer. The mourners were mostly old comrades, come to pay their respects.

"Many of these people have not spoken to one another in ages," Marta told Claire. "Political divisions have turned friends into bitter enemies. You have to understand, these people lived for politics. Each international crisis — the Hungarian uprising, the invasion of Czechoslovakia, revelations of Stalinist terror — swept through our group like a deadly virus destroying in its path friendships, love affairs, even marriages. There are people here today who still cannot bear to be in the same room, that's how deep the old wounds run. They only meet at gravesides, reconciled for a brief moment in shared grief. At Bruno's funeral the crowd was even larger and I saw people then who had avoided us for years. Awful, isn't it?"

Claire looked at the mourners who showed no trace of the fury Marta described. They were mostly elderly men and women, some with small patches of tricolor on their lapels, many carrying flowers that would be strewn on the grave. They stood singly, or in small groups, sheltered under black umbrellas to protect themselves from the persistent light rain. Some were supported by middle-aged children who ignored the feuds separating their parents and exchanged greetings over the old people's heads.

Claire remembered how solitary Gertrude had appeared in her spotless, silent flat. Now people thronged around her grave. There were several speeches which threatened at moments to revive old political wounds, but somehow each speaker remembered the occasion and pulled back. Gertrude's son read a letter his mother had left, asking her family and friends to forgive her and to remember her in happier days. Claire saw several of the mourners wipe away tears as they listened to Gertrude's words.

Despite the rain, people continued to cluster in small groups after the ceremony was over. Claire saw Marta moving from one group to another, embracing old friends. Henri, her companion, followed closely, his manner reserved as always, standing a little apart each time she stopped to greet someone, yet discreetly conveying his claim on Marta.

Claire, waiting for Marta, found her thoughts drifting back to the day when she and her father had buried Dolly. Despite the bright sunshine, it had been a bitterly cold Montréal winter morning. Only a handful of mourners, mostly Dolly's colleagues, had been brave enough to accompany the hearse to the cemetery. That day, there had been no lingering at the graveside. A cruel wind and icy temperatures made it dangerous to remain in the open, and the burial had been hasty, almost furtive. Claire, numbed by the cold and the shock of her mother's sudden death, had been unable to shed any tears. Now, at the funeral of someone she scarcely knew, she was overcome by a wave of sorrow so intense, tears streamed down her face. People standing nearby looked at her with curiosity, wondering who she was. She turned away from them, unable to control her weeping. Her tears, coming so long after Dolly's death, finally eased the constriction that had clutched at her heart, preventing the natural flow of feeling for her mother. The anger she had been nurturing against Dolly since Gertrude's revelation — even longer — had turned to grief at last.

Henri drove them back to Marta's flat. When he offered to come in, Marta said she wanted to rest and suggested Henri could use a nap as well.

"I am tired," Marta said when they were alone, "but I sent Henri home because I wanted to talk to you. I have read Gertrude's letter and I know about her conversation with you. She had no right to tell you about Bruno and Dolly. I can't even begin to understand her motives and I'm not sure I want to. Given her state of mind, I will try to forgive her. Perhaps in some way she has done us a service. It hasn't been easy for me to avoid your questions. I was trying to protect you, knowing the truth would hurt. When I saw you crying at the cemetery, I realized I had to set things straight. Gertrude, after all, was only a distant observer to the events. Yes, I confided in her at the time, but she couldn't possibly convey to you the feelings involved."

Claire looked away from Marta. She felt drained after the funeral and again, as with Gertrude, she had to fight her rising panic. It was becoming easier to regain control, she noticed, while Marta busied herself making coffee. Marta's doctors had forbidden her caffeine, but she indulged her addiction occasionally "for medicinal purposes."

Now that the longed-for conversation with Marta was about to take place, Claire didn't feel ready. Marta also hesitated, sipping her coffee quietly for a minute, relishing the forbidden brew. The coffee seemed to give her strength and she resumed. "I wish I could make you understand how things were for all of us. To tell you the truth, I find it difficult to recapture the emotions of that time. It was all so long ago. Bruno, Dolly and I, we were close friends. Your mother was a very attractive woman and she had that kind of warmth and charm that drew people to her. Even Louise, who was going through a difficult adolescence at the time, adored her. I think she would have wanted Dolly to be her mother. Bruno was not a great womanizer. Politics was his true mistress, but I knew he was attracted to Dolly. That kind of sexual tension often occurs between people who like each other and spend a great deal of time together."

Marta paused for a moment, and went on. "I hope this doesn't shock you, but Jacques and I were once drawn to each other. I tell you this to give you some background. In our circle infidelity was not considered a serious transgression. After all, we were committed to being anti-bourgeois and we saw possessiveness as part of the stifling conventions of marriage. Of course there was jealousy and bitter recrimination, but we fought hard to root out these vestiges of our traditional upbringing. I am not by any means suggesting we were wildly promiscuous. We simply tried not to attach too much importance to monogamy. It may sound strange to you, but I believe it made our relationships far more durable than they are today. Sexual affairs rarely became grounds for divorce."

Claire didn't really want to hear about Marta's infidelities, she thought, remembering Bruno, but she had brought this on herself with her probing and so she kept her expression neutral while she listened.

"In Dolly's case, politics, of course, had nothing to do with it," Marta continued. "She kept her wildness and passion for her work. In all other ways, she was surprisingly conventional. I don't think her marriage to your father was a particularly happy one. Temperamentally, they were simply too different. I had warned her before she married him, but she felt she needed the stability he offered to pursue her art. I suppose it worked for a while. She had her work, she had you, and she seemed satisfied. She certainly never complained about her life. The last time she came to Paris, I had to go to Switzerland. It was only natural that she and Bruno continued seeing each other. I remember feeling guilty about leaving her on her own and I urged Bruno to keep an eye on her. Bruno had to be reminded to do those kinds of things. Or so I thought. You see, I was always the practical one in our family.

"It's difficult for me to talk about the dreadful day when I found her lying half-dead in a studio not far from here on rue Charlot. I wanted to kill the man who had left her there to bleed to death. Then I learned it was Bruno. I remember screaming at him, How could you have allowed her to end up in the hands of a butcher? Her life was in danger for days. I sat by her side willing her to live and at the same time overwhelmed by my own feelings of rage and betrayal. What I couldn't express to her, I let out on Bruno. It was easier to blame him than Dolly, too ill for punishment."

Marta's face suddenly looked ravaged and old and Claire had an inkling of the hurt these distant events still caused her. She put her hand over Marta's and said, "I'm sorry." It sounded lame, but she couldn't think of anything else. It wasn't easy to apologize for your mother's adultery.

Marta did not respond. "We're coming to the part affecting you," was all she said. "When Dolly began to recover, she was inconsolable. She blamed herself for everything. I was forced to put my own feelings aside in the face of her wild, incoherent grief. She was so tormented the doctors at the hospital feared she might be suicidal. A staff psychologist told me it was the abortion that troubled her most. I must admit I found it hard to comprehend the intensity of her grief. In our circle many women had had abortions. We were constantly fighting to have abortion legalized. As I sat with her in the hospital room listening to her ravings I began to understand. Somehow she believed the child she had killed was you. It's crazy, I know, but in her anguished state she felt you were the one who had been torn away from her. It was as if the child she had destroyed was a replica of you and she couldn't bear its loss. In any case, that was the way I interpreted her suffering. Only the loss of a child can cause such pain."

Claire saw herself suddenly joining a line of grieving women stretching back to the beginning of time and thought, I'm not ready for this. She forced her attention back to what Marta was saying.

"I tried to comfort her, even though my own hurt was still raw. I told her about the abortion I'd had and how in a few months she would forget all about hers. I still believe she would have recovered eventually. In time, I forgave Bruno. Things were never the same between us but our ties remained strong. We shared many happy moments together in the years that followed. I also forgave Dolly, but I don't think she ever forgave herself. When I learned about her death, I couldn't look at Bruno, although I knew he was in no way responsible. We mourned her separately, unable to share our grief."

Marta's eyes were now filled with tears and Claire found herself sobbing for the second time that day. Marta, who was usually not given to physical demonstration, put her arms around Claire. "It's good to cry for her, my darling," she said, hugging Claire. "But when you've stopped crying you must remember how much she loved you. That kind of love makes you one of the lucky ones of this world. Never forget that."

Suddenly Claire wanted to tell Marta about the baby, but something held her back. Her reluctance troubled her. Did it mean she was wavering, still unsure that she wanted the child? She didn't think so, but she could not bring herself to speak.

Marta went off for a nap and Claire moved to the sofa in the living room. She fell asleep and awoke still tired, but wonderfully peaceful. What had passed out of her was the maddening restlessness, the constant need to know about Dolly. The anger she had felt against Dolly since Gertrude's revelations was gone. The grief had waned as well. What if that bus hadn't swerved into Dolly's path? she wondered. Would she have found her way back to her work? Perhaps her misery had been so deep, she had wanted to die. Claire dismissed the thought. She had every reason to believe in Dolly's strength and in the healing power of the work itself. The silent figures emerging from her skilled hands would have eased her anguish in time. Her poor mother, she thought sadly, had never been given the chance to find out. By choosing to believe in Dolly's ultimate recovery, Claire felt she was giving her that chance.

Later, when Adrian came home, she was ready to tell him about Dolly. Dolly's secret had already lost the jagged edges that had ripped her emotions apart only days ago. She had found a place for it in her heart where it rested quietly, sending out occasional signals of distress. But the worst was over and she was able to tell her story calmly.

"What a dreadful mess," Adrian said. "Did you have any inkling of this? Was that why you were so persistent?"

"I don't know," Claire answered truthfully. "I knew something had happened, but I never allowed myself to speculate about what it might be."

"I'm sorry I doubted you," Adrian said, putting his arms around her to comfort her.

It gave Claire no satisfaction to hear him say that. She didn't want to be right, to think of herself as one of Lucinda's "spiritual" people, blessed with the dubious gift of premonition. She didn't trust the dark side of her imagination.

Later, when she awoke during the night, Adrian was not beside her. She went looking for him and found him sitting in the dark living room.

"I can't sleep," he said when he saw her. "I keep thinking about what you told me. About your mother, and what happened to her."

Claire sat down beside him and took his hand. "It's all right," she said. "I'm glad I found out. I always prefer to know the truth, no matter what it is."

"I know," he said, squeezing her hand. "It's one of your admirable traits. But it changes everything."

"How do you mean?"

"I can't talk to you about having an abortion now. It wouldn't be fair. Perhaps it never was." Claire held her breath, waiting for him to continue.

He turned to face her. "You see, I thought we had a pact. An inviolable pact. When you told me you were pregnant, I felt betrayed. I blamed you. It was probably unfair, but there it is. It seemed to me there was only one way to put things right. To go back to what we had. Oh Claire, I really loved what we had."

She heard the regret in his voice and her heart sank. Was he saying it was over? She waited, dreading his next words.

"But your story . . . . It made me see we will never be the same again. If I insist on the abortion, you will surely come to hate me, and if we go ahead and have the child . . ."

She sat very still, waiting for him to finish the sentence. Instead, he moved closer, so that their faces were inches apart, but she could still not read his eyes. "Do you want the baby?" he asked softly.

"Yes," she said firmly, "very much." At that moment her doubts seemed very distant.

He pulled her into his arms, his lips brushing her ear. "I don't want to lose you."

"You won't," she whispered back. "You'll never lose me, no matter what happens." She felt strong comforting

183

Adrian, capable of making her promises come true. She took his hand and led him back to their bed. They began to make love, the best kind of love, fueled by abstinence, regret and forgiveness. Claire was astonished by the intensity of her responses. It must be the effect of all those newly churning hormones, she thought, and gave herself up to pleasure as if she had never known it before.

Just before she fell asleep, she silently thanked Dolly for Adrian's change of heart. She knew it was a reluctant, half-hearted change, but at least they were together again. She counted on her new powers to bring him around.

TWENTY-ONE

Adrian was gone by the time Claire awoke the next morning. He had left a note in the pocket of her dressing gown. Three words: "I love you," written in his neat handwriting. She wished he had made some reference to their new understanding, but that was probably asking too much.

To her surprise, Marta was waiting for her in the kitchen. She felt herself being scrutinized so closely, she blushed, but all Marta said was that she was counting on Claire to accompany her on a visit to Jacques' new home. "I know I'm taking advantage of you, but I don't think I can face it alone," she said. "Those kinds of institutions are so depressing, particularly at my age when you realize all that separates you from the people inside is some fragile synapse or osteoporotic bone which may snap at any time."

It was not like Marta to dwell on her frailty; Claire agreed to go along although she had planned to take the train to Dormay to reshoot scenes that continued to elude her. The countess expressed disappointment when Claire called to postpone her visit, and Claire promised to come the following day.

The institution Gertrude had selected for Jacques was located in a nineteenth-century villa on the outskirts of Paris. From the outside, surrounded by a pleasant garden, it looked far more attractive than similar facilities Claire had seen in Montréal. Once they passed through the ornate carved doors, however, the smell that hit her — a stale mixture of food, disinfectant and medicinal odors — and the immobile figures arranged around a large television set, were just as dismal. She was glad to hear that Jacques had been taken outside to wait for them. "He becomes very angry if we try keep him in his room," a male nurse explained. "So we let him stay outdoors as much as possible."

They found Jacques with an attendant in the garden at the back of the house. The attendant sat on a bench reading a newspaper while Jacques inspected the lawn with intense concentration. He was down on his hands and knees, peering closely at the new grass, and gave no sign of noticing their arrival.

"He's looking for weeds," the attendant said as they drew near. "He makes a hell of a mess sometimes, but it keeps the old bugger happy. Jacques, *mon vieux,* you've got visitors," he shouted with a familiarity that made Marta flinch. When Jacques failed to respond, the attendant got up and brought him over. He seemed willing to follow the attendant, although he continued to look back at the task he had been forced to abandon. Up close, they could see he was wearing pajamas with a loose robe over them. The belt of his robe was knotted into a tie under his pajama collar, adding an odd note of elegance to his appearance.

"Why is he dressed in pajamas?" Marta demanded angrily. "And where are his ties? He looks like a prisoner or an inmate in an insane asylum."

"Oh, we get him dressed up when we can," the attendant replied evenly. "Today is not one of his better days, but he can be a regular dandy at times. It was his idea to turn the belt into a tie. He must have been quite a ladies' man in his day. Isn't that right, Jacques?"

Jacques ignored the question. He looked in anticipation at the two women. "Have you come to take me away?" he asked with the eagerness of a child.

Marta took his hand. "It's me, Jacques," she said, "I've brought you chocolates. Your favorite kind."

"Have you come to take me on a trip?" he repeated, ignoring the box held out to him. "I've been ready since this morning." The eagerness was now replaced by a sense of urgency. "Let's go. It will be a long journey."

"Not today," Marta said, taking his hand in hers and gently caressing it. "Maybe next time." The look of tenderness on Marta's face made Claire feel she was intruding on a private moment. How awful it must be for Marta to see her old lover so diminished.

Jacques smiled at Marta with no hint of recognition and slowly pulled his hand back. A moment later, he had resumed his search for weeds and stray twigs, their presence forgotten.

"Shame on you," the attendant scolded him. "These nice ladies brought you chocolates and they've come all the way from Paris to see you and you run away. Where are your manners?"

"Leave him alone," Marta said sharply. "He's not a child. You must not speak to him like that."

The young man looked up, startled. "You've got the wrong idea, lady. We're great pals, you know. Isn't that right, Jacques? I'm the only one he allows to bathe him. You should see the fuss he kicks up with the others."

"I'm sorry," Marta said, chastened. "Please take good care of him." She slipped several bills into the attendant's hand.

"Don't worry about a thing," he said, pocketing the money. "I'll make sure he's happy here."

They watched silently for a few minutes as Jacques worked eagerly on his self-assigned task. Now and then finding something on the ground that puzzled him, he stopped, waiting until some impulse prompted him to carry the foreign object to one of the several piles he had amassed. He seemed content and oblivious to everyone around him.

"It's quite a job cleaning that mess up after he gets through," the attendant explained. "I push the leaves and the stones back on the grass, and the next day he starts all over again. One thing's for sure, he gets plenty of exercise around here."

"I can't stand it another minute," Marta said to Claire, pulling her arm. "Let's get out of here."

"God, Gertrude should have killed Jacques as well as herself," Marta added when they were back in the car. "Thank goodness he doesn't know what's happening to him. It's a feeble consolation, but one I must hold on to if I'm ever to visit him again. Not that my coming makes much difference. But we do these things for ourselves, don't we?"

They drove back in near silence, lost in private thoughts. Claire remembered Gertrude's strange phone call and the revelations that followed. She wondered if Gertrude had been motivated by a desire to wound Marta — a sort of final settling of accounts before her suicide. The love affairs in Marta's circle seemed to reverberate long after the passion had died. No wonder Marta looked sad and tired.

"I have some good news," Claire said, hoping to raise Marta's spirit. "I'm pregnant."

Marta's expression brightened immediately. "How wonderful, darling. That *is* good news. And Adrian, how is he taking it?"

"He's adjusting." Loyalty prevented her from revealing Adrian's initial negative response and the reason for his half-hearted turnabout. "He needs time to get used to the idea. We didn't plan this, you know."

"Well, that's fortunate. Who knows if you would have ever gotten around to it on your own. You are both far too organized for your own good. A baby will change all that. That's what's so wonderful about having children. They will not be put off the way a lover or a friend can be put off. Their needs are so immediate, you have to respond on the spot."

"That is precisely what Adrian dreads."

"In the abstract, yes. But I promise you, once the child is there, he will dote on it. Bruno was like that. Louise was the only one who could tear him away from his work. I must

188

confess, there were times I longed for Louise's power over her father. You'll see, Adrian will be no different."

"I hope you're right."

"Don't worry," Marta said, patting her hand. "He's bound to be a better father than Rousseau." Claire burst out laughing and she was pleased to see Marta laughing with her.

After they had parked the car near Marta's flat, Claire noticed Adrian on the terrace of the nearby café. To her amazement, she saw he was with Marcel, and she walked over to join them. She was dying to hear about his escapade with Sophie.

Marcel's exaggerated expression of contrition when he greeted her made her want to laugh. Folding his hands as if in prayer and hanging his head, he said, "I have been the worst fool there is, Claire, an old fool in love. You, my beautiful Claire, an ardent reader of Rousseau, will understand my plight. The great philosopher was also rendered ludicrous by passion." Marcel closed his eyes and breathed deeply as if to emphasize the strength of his feelings. The performance was interrupted by a violent fit of coughing that made him reach for his inhalator. Claire looked at Adrian to see his response: Adrian was in no mood to forgive Marcel. He seemed to be fighting the kind of revulsion she had often felt for Marcel. Marcel looked imploringly at her again and she understood she was being asked to intercede with Adrian.

When Marcel could speak again, the tale he told of his ill-fated romance with Sophie was indeed worthy of the philosopher's worst romantic disasters. Several weeks in the company of Marcel had turned Sophie from an adoring student to a young woman who despised him. Their affair had really been over before it began, since it had never been consummated, despite his passion for her. This admission caused him to hang his head in shame. But he was willing to reveal further humiliation in the hope of forgiveness.

Only pride and an unwillingness to admit her folly to her parents had kept Sophie at Marcel's side, each passing day intensifying her contempt for him. Finally, unable to bear her scorn, he had asked her to leave. He had even written a letter to her parents to assure them of the innocent nature of his contact with their daughter.

"I know you will find this hard to believe, but the whole adventure was Sophie's idea. She said there was so much I could teach her. In return, she offered to help with the manuscript I was preparing. She was willing to be my chauffeur, to type my notes, to look after me, just for the chance to discuss ideas with me. I still can't understand what happened. Was it some cruel game she invented to torture me? Oh God, how well she succeeded."

TWENTY-TWO

In the days that followed, Adrian's anger waned and he eventually forgave Marcel. He could not do otherwise. Even Sophie's parents agreed to see Marcel again. Sophie herself corroborated Marcel's version while keeping her distance. An abject and subdued Marcel was back again among his old friends.

Now that Adrian had found Marcel and Marta was reunited with Antoine, Claire was free to resume her work for the countess. Despite her uncertainty when she had accepted the assignment, the project had assumed a life of its own. The hundreds of photographs the countess had taken of the Dormay estate over the years crowded Claire's own efforts and challenged her to continual attempts at refining her work.

In the past her struggle with her subject matter had continued in the darkroom. When she positioned her negative in the enlarger, the attraction she found in a specific scene recurred even more intensely. Now she had to forego this darkroom. The obstetrician she had consulted at the American Hospital had confirmed Adrian's warning and advised her to avoid using chemicals in the confined space. She relied instead on a lab she found on Boulevard Voltaire. With the help of a cooperative technician, she tried to achieve a balance between the small telling motif — the shadows in the stone drapery of a statue, for example — and the full sweep of a broad perspective. Detail had always been paramount in her work; now she had to use it to convey the vast spaces and endless vistas of the countess' gardens.

The landscape she had tried to fix in her lens became more elusive and changeable with each new set of prints and she found herself obsessed by the work, her mind sifting through images even while she slept. The prints she produced began to exert their own mysterious power, eliciting in her the same pleasant sense of dissociation she had experienced when walking in the gardens. She had no idea if this disconcerting effect would be perceptible to anyone else; until now she had kept her work to herself.

When she finally obtained a satisfying set of prints, she carefully packaged the work and brought it to the countess. Waiting for her reaction, Claire felt as nervous as a beginner; there was more at stake here than she realized. The Countess de Guersaird kept her in suspense during a long period as she silently studied the work. Finally, she looked up and Claire saw her eyes glistening with tears. "My dear, you have made an old woman very happy. You have shown an appreciation of this place I would never have believed possible in a stranger. What I find remarkable is that you have made me see my beloved home with fresh eyes. Somehow, in these images the familiar elements I have known all my life have been altered. Everything is the same and yet different." Claire could not believe how happy these words made her feel.

Later, over tea, the countess insisted Claire's work must be displayed and suggested it be shown at the château during the fourteenth of July celebration. "We always have a great party on Bastille Day. The grounds are turned over to the public and we set up long tables in the courtyard for a communal feast. I want you to invite as many people as you like. Your work deserves to be admired. We no longer send out invitations, but I still have some from previous years. You may take them. Just change the date."

Adrian and Claire's stay in Paris was drawing to an end and Adrian agreed that the countess' party would be a fitting way to bring their friends together one last time. The countess' invitation, with the family crest which Claire had photographed over the main gateway, was duly delivered to Marta, Zoé and Simon, Marcel, and Sophie's parents,

Gilbert and Anne-Marie. Sophie herself was vacationing in Greece, following her disastrous escapade with Marcel. Just as well, Claire thought, witnessing Marcel's delight with the invitation. "A country picnic on the grounds of the château with my dearest friends. What a delightful prospect. I must say you've had unusual luck in penetrating French society. Of course, Adrian's reputation is very high in certain circles."

Claire wished she had the strength of character to resist reminding Marcel he owed his invitation to her friendship with Madame de Guersaird and not to Adrian's reputation. But she didn't; Marcel's penitent expression following her reprimand almost made her regret her pettiness.

Surprisingly, Marta was hardly more difficult to persuade. "I am curious to meet this woman who has taken up so much of your time," she conceded, examining the invitation. Since their conversation following Gertrude's funeral, Marta had become more agreeable and no longer made sharp pronouncements about Claire's activities. "Perhaps I'll take Antoine along. The boy is very interested in photography, as I told you, and I want him to see your work. Henri will probably not come. He dislikes crowds and hates missing his afternoon nap."

Plans for the meal and what each person would bring were the subject of many conversations in the days that ensued. The countess had made it clear that her reduced circumstances prevented her from treating all comers. Claire was just as glad; the few meals she had taken at the château during her visits had been downright sparse. The countess, she had quickly learned, always welcomed any little treat Claire brought along and ate it with appreciative gusto.

Claire had intended to tell Zoé about the baby before the picnic; there would be too many people about during the festivities. She had thought the news important enough to require a meeting, but when Zoé called to say a patient had cancelled, Claire decided to seize the moment. "I was hoping to hear from you. There's something I'm dying to tell you."

"I should be working on a paper or returning telephone messages, instead of goofing off with you." Zoé sounded grumpy, reproachful, but Claire understood that Zoé's call was an invitation for diversion.

"Never mind. Wait till you hear what I have to say."

"It better not be anything upsetting. The stories I've heard this morning from the patients who did show up have left me with a very dim view of human nature."

"Will you stop grumbling and listen for a moment? I'm pregnant."

"Oh my God. What wonderful news, Claire. I'm so excited for you." But Zoé didn't sound excited. Her voice was heavy with weariness and regret. "I envy you, starting over again. Everything seems to be unraveling in my life."

This was not the response Claire had expected, but concern for her friend overcame disappointment. "What's wrong? Has something happened?"

"I might as well tell you," Zoé replied with unusual reluctance. "Simon has decided to leave us."

"Oh no!" Claire gasped. "I can't believe it."

"Don't be shocked. We're not talking of a permanent separation, at least not yet."

Zoé's feeble reassurance failed to calm Claire. For years, she had thought of Zoé and Simon as a couple to emulate. Despite their recent troubles, she had continued to believe in the solidity of their marriage. Now they were separating. She tried to suppress her dismay, remembering that her friend needed her support. "My poor Zoé, how awful for both of you. What brought you to this decision?"

"We've been drifting apart for years, too busy with day-to-day life to notice the signs. The tension became unbearable finally. I can hardly say anything to Simon these days without upsetting him. His depression is getting worse and it's weighing heavily upon all of us, particularly the children. He sees how his moods are affecting us and the guilt he feels only increases his unhappiness. So he's decided to leave us for a while. Perhaps he needs the solitude to sort things out. You know, I'm not indifferent to his difficulties, even if I don't always express my concern to him. To tell you the truth, what saddens me is that I'm actually relieved to be free of his misery for a while. Away from Simon, I may be able to feel more sympathy for him."

"I'm so sorry," Claire said. "You know how much I care for both of you."

"I do, but I'm the one who should be sorry for spoiling your happy news with our troubles. I'll make it up to you, I promise. Now, I must go. I can hear my next patient's soulful sighs in the waiting room."

After Zoé hung up, Claire thought about how much she had always depended on the success of Zoé and Simon's marriage. In the years before she met Adrian, whenever a love affair had ended badly, she had been comforted to think of Zoé and Simon and the good feeling she had when she was with them. For years their marriage had been the gauge by which all other relationships, including her own, were measured. If Zoé and Simon's marriage was breaking up, then perhaps she and Adrian were in jeopardy as well. God knows, their quarrel over her pregnancy had made that prospect very real.

TWENTY-THREE

"In all the years I've lived in France, I can't remember it ever raining on Bastille Day," Marta assured Claire. But gray skies and rainy days persisted as the date of the party approached. "Of course, ever since Chernobyl the weather has become very quirky. So I really don't know what to tell you."

By now Claire had acquired the habit of dialing the Paris weather number before heading out of the house. Since the message changed several times during the day, she became familiar with the repertoire of musical interludes preceding each new bulletin. A violin rendition of "My Way" seemed to be the most frequent offering as June turned to July. The message itself, detailing weather conditions in the different regions of France, gave her the illusion of physical intimacy with the entire country: Brittany, the Beauce, the hills of Normandy, the basins of the Seine and Loire, the Massif Central, the temperate South guarded by the Pyrenees on the west and the Alps on the east — each region with its distinct climate seemed as close as the adjacent *arrondissement*.

On the day of the countess' party, the weather bulletin offered a new song — *"La Vie en Rose"* — and a cheery forecast: sunshine and warm temperatures would prevail from the North Sea to the Mediterranean, just as Marta had predicted.

They had decided to avoid the holiday traffic on the roads and take the train. Henri, Marta's much-maligned companion, insisted he would put up with the inconvenience of crowds and miss his nap this once for Marta's sake. Marta, for all her complaining, appeared pleased. She looked particularly smart in a dark blue blazer over a soft silk blouse, and Claire suspected she had dressed as much for the countess as for the occasion. Antoine, the prodigal grandson, also agreed to come, and happily followed his grandmother's instructions for packing the food hamper.

At the station, they found Marcel, still contrite, but looking unusually polished in a maroon jacket Claire had never seen before — no doubt a relic of Sophie's efforts to spruce him up. He had already met up with Zoé and Simon, and was clinging to them, Zoé whispered to Claire, as if they were his parents. Their own two children, Christophe and Juliette, appeared amused by Marcel's helplessness. Zoé's family seemed to be in harmony on this festive day, Claire was happy to see, and she hugged them with delight. After they had all kissed and been kissed on both cheeks, a lengthy salutation involving nine people, they boarded the train, eager to begin their celebration.

The train was crowded, but they managed to find seats and space for their food baskets. A note of holiday cheer prevailed in the car, making everyone accept the crowding and the noise with good humor. An Arab family, the women in traditional dress, looked curiously upon the festive goings-on and laughed shyly behind their hands as wine bottles appeared and bits of song traveled from one group to another. Several Poles announced their presence by singing songs in their own language which the French travelers accompanied with enthusiastic humming.

"A day like this brings out the best in everyone," Marta said, surveying the scene with amusement. "It's hard to believe when you see this sort of camaraderie how xenophobic the French can be."

At the station taxis waited to convey them to the château where the party seemed well under way. Thomas, who admitted them, confirmed that people from nearby villages had been arriving since dawn. The Countess de Guersaird, seated on the terrace under a tattered umbrella shading her from the sun, looked impressively regal as she surveyed the vista of lawns and pools stretching before her and the people beginning to gather there. She had abandoned her usual black attire and was dressed for the occasion in brilliant colors, topped by a large straw hat adorned with red, white, and blue silk poppies. "*À votre santé, Comtesse,*" an occasional early reveler shouted beneath the terrace, holding up a glass or a bottle of wine, while the countess returned the greeting with a gracious wave of her hand.

"What a sight," Marta whispered in Claire's ear. "Peasants celebrating the Revolution by toasting an aristocrat. Their ancestors would turn over in their graves."

The countess appeared genuinely delighted by the arrival of Claire and her friends, and even Marta was charmed by the warmth of their reception. The elegant chatelaine rose to greet them, murmuring a personal word or two to each guest as she offered her hand, making a particular point of putting young Antoine at ease by admiring the intricately embroidered cap he wore. "I adore youth," she said, smiling fondly at the three young people who seemed awed by their unusual-looking hostess.

Marcel, nearly overcome when it was his turn to be presented, kissed the countess' hand and proclaimed his admiration for the château and its grounds. Claire and Adrian exchanged a conspiratorial smile, remembering Marcel's skepticism on the train when Adrian had told him the gardens at Château de Dormay were attributed to Le Nôtre. "Every two-bit château claims Le Nôtre for its gardens. Most so-called Le Nôtre gardens are about as authentic as the Vuitton bags shopgirls carry these days." In the presence of the property's aristocratic owner, however, Marcel's reservations vanished. He poured forth his appreciation, extolling Le Nôtre's use of scale, balance and proportion to such exquisite effect.

The countess, using a cane, adroitly maneuvered her small frame past Marcel's awkward bulk. "You must begin the day by viewing our exhibition," she said, leading the way inside. " We call it *Hommage à Rousseau.*" Dutifully, the party followed their hostess as she made her way slowly along the sides of the long table in the dining hall.

"It has been a long time since this table was used for anything worthwhile," the countess said. "I'm delighted to find a purpose for it again. Your wife is a very talented woman," she added, turning to Adrian, "but you know that already, of course. I think she's a conjurer at heart. Just look at these images. Everything appears as it is, quite ordinary at first glance. Yet each scene is pervaded by a feeling of loss, a reminder of the perishable nature of all gardens. It's as if she had read my heart. That's sorcery, don't you think?"

While Adrian hesitated, trying to find an appropriate response, Marcel, standing near him, rushed to his aid. "The camera is a fluid way of encountering that other reality, a way of seeing what we ourselves perceive only as shadowy sentiments . . ." Claire slipped out of the room, not wishing to hear the rest of Marcel's analysis. She had been uncomfortable for some minutes listening to her friends praise her work, and Marcel's comments gave her the final push.

"You're afraid you've revealed too much of yourself," Zoé said, following her, "and you have. These photographs are as much about you as they are about the landscapes. They're really magnificent. But you needn't worry. For most people art is a mirror, not a window. A self-mirroring esthetic that involves finding your own reflection. Relax, your secrets are safe."

Claire laughed a little uneasily. Zoé's perceptions sometimes cut too close to the bone. "I have no secrets from you."

"I certainly hope that's not true. It would make you very boring, which of course you are not. Looking at your beautiful work, I thought how proud your mother would have been. It's a pity she did not live to see you carry on her tradition, but I'm convinced her talent lives on through you. And, as you will soon discover, this is the most wonderful

199

part about having children. They become your messengers into the future, carrying forward certain traits — a tone of voice, an eye for symmetry, or an intolerance for tomatoes, for example — that persist long after you're gone. When I look at my children, I find traces of my parents, grandparents, relatives I know only through description. It can be unnerving, but ultimately it expands your own existence."

"How profound you've become," Claire said, happy to see Zoé in such good form. Zoé was right about the debt Claire owed her mother. She had been a stubborn, difficult child, but she was grateful for Dolly's gifts now: her keen eye, her odd sense of composition, her ability to temper passion with discipline. Was this cycle of rejection and regret inevitable between children and parents? Dying young, Dolly had missed out on so many pleasures, among them the satisfaction of seeing her obstinate daughter's change of heart.

Hunger soon put an end to the impromptu *vernissage*. The countess declined Claire's invitation to share their meal, explaining she was expecting her son and his family. They left her, ensconced once again in her high perch overlooking her domain, and set off to look for Gilbert and Anne-Marie, whom they had arranged to meet on the grounds.

Finding them was not easy. The presence of the crowds disoriented Claire, who was used to having this place to herself. Finally, the right statue was found, with Gilbert and Anne-Marie beside it as arranged. Claire, being the one most familiar with the terrain, led the way. She had in mind an out-of-the-way spot overlooking a stream, ideal for their picnic. When they reached it after a short walk, she was surprised to see other families already camped beneath the great row of chestnut trees reflected in the nearby pools of water.

"Never mind," Zoé said. "On a day like this you're supposed to be part of the throng. Once you're back in

Canada, you'll have all the empty space you can want. Europe is crowded. It must make you feel claustrophobic at times."

"Not at all," Claire said as she added the contents of her hamper to the communal meal. "That's precisely what I like about the Old World. When people are forced to live cheek by jowl in small well-defined areas, their sense of civility towards one another becomes more critical. Otherwise, their lives would be a misery. Look at those people over there," she said, pointing to a large family nearby. "You see how careful they are to pick up after themselves? Even the children are being restrained from what I can see."

"It's true," Antoine said with enthusiasm as he helped himself to some bread and cheese from Anne-Marie's larder. "We are trained in obedience like dogs or circus animals. Everything in our upbringing is intended to make us suppress any lively impulse. When we leave the family, the state and its bureaucracy run our lives. With all this repression, no wonder the whole country is permanently fixated on its digestive problems."

"Come and sit beside your grandmother," Marta said, pulling him down beside her. "It's clear no one has managed to repress either your tongue or your appetite."

Christophe, who had taken a liking to Antoine during the train ride, rose to his new friend's defense. "You really have to leave the country to realize how tyrannical French families are."

"Especially French fathers, right?" Simon said, teasing his son good-naturedly. "Christophe participated in an exchange program last year. When he returned after living with a Canadian family for a month, he found us very wanting."

"There's no ham in this, I hope?" Antoine asked reaching for a sandwich.

"Are you a vegetarian?" Zoé responded, handing him an egg, olive and tomato sandwich.

"No, I've become a Muslim. I eat meat but no pork."

201

Silence followed Antoine's startling announcement until Marta offered a word of explanation: "Antoine has become the disciple of a Muslim cleric who has persuaded him to give up not only ham but drugs. It seems to be working." She spoke calmly, but alone with Claire she had confessed her dismay about her grandson's conversion. "When I think how hard my generation fought to free itself from the oppressive controls imposed on our lives by religion, it pains me to see Antoine eagerly embrace the restrictions of a religion he barely understands. Antoine will probably not remain a Muslim for long, at least I hope not, but there's no denying the willingness of his generation to follow every new 'spiritual' Messiah. We might as well be back in the Dark Ages."

As if to confirm Marta's suspicions, Claire noticed Juliette, a fervent supporter of Muslim rights, looking at Antoine with interest. During the train ride she had pointedly ignored him and her brother. Now, she made her way over to Antoine's side and the two were soon talking quietly apart from the others.

Claire turned her attention to a group of children playing nearby with a soccer ball. For all the supposed restrictions of their upbringing, they played as wildly and energetically as any children she had ever seen. Boys and girls ran back and forth in a frenzy of excitement that seemed to exact a victim every few minutes as one child after another collapsed on the grass in paroxysms of laughter and squealing. Claire wondered whether she had ever played so freely. She doubted it. She saw herself more like the little girl sitting at the edge of the makeshift soccer field playing with her purse, seemingly oblivious of the other children and their rough game. The purse and the child looked familiar. It couldn't possibly be the same girl who had approached her at the Gustave-Moreau museum, eager to display the contents of her new shoulder bag. Yet this child had that same quality of self-containment, unusual in one so small.

Movement around her interrupted Claire's thoughts. She looked up to see two small boys running past her yelling something, but their words fused into an incomprehensible sound. "What's happening?" she asked Zoé, who had jumped to her feet.

"I don't know. They're calling for help. I can't make out anything else."

They were all standing now, watching the progress of the boys. The other children had abandoned their game and were running with them. Antoine took off after them. Halfway down the field he turned and, still running, cupped his hands around his mouth and shouted: "The kids were fishing. One of them fell into the river."

Antoine's voice seemed to mobilize people. Several men were now running in the direction from which the boys had come. Their own little group seemed frozen momentarily between the two currents running in opposite directions. Claire remembered how calm the river had always appeared, but what if the boy couldn't swim? The waiting seemed unbearable and she found herself running with the others towards the river. Another shout now moved through the crowd, reaching her after a few seconds. "He's been found, he's been found," people repeated to those behind them.

The running stopped and an uneasy stillness replaced the confusion of the last few minutes. Claire felt as if they were all holding their breath. A young man about Antoine's age came into sight carrying the child in his arms. The boy appeared lifeless.

In an instant Gilbert had taken charge of the child and placed him on the ground. Anne-Marie moved quietly to his side to help him. The tension was intolerable as they watched in silence while Gilbert and Anne-Marie worked on the small body. With rhythmic, precise movements Gilbert pressed the child's chest while Anne-Marie regularly breathed into his mouth. They lost track of time, their eyes fixed on the repeated life-saving motions, their own breathing shallow while they waited for the child's to resume. The only sound came from the weeping of a woman kneeling near the child, his mother. The terrifying anguish in her face made Claire look away. She heard a cry of triumph and turned back to see the child stirring. He coughed, and water and slime spurted from his mouth. He was alive.

"He's going to be all right," Gilbert announced, rising to his feet. For the first time since Claire had met him, he looked exhausted. "I'll take him back to the clinic to check him over, but he's going to be fine." The grateful mother embraced both Gilbert and the young man who had pulled her child out of the water. All around her people were cheering and Claire felt her eyes fill with tears.

The crowd dispersed quickly as people drifted back to their blankets and hampers and settled down among family and friends to resume the pleasures of the day. The desperate, glorious moment when they had breathed as one and hoped with one mind had passed. They acknowledged it with smiles of relief and assurances that yes, the little boy had been very lucky. Mothers kept a closer eye on their children and hugged them a little tighter when they came running for comfort or nourishment. Relief seemed to whet appetites and fresh bottles of wine were uncorked and glasses raised to celebrate the happy dénouement.

The excitement gave way to a pleasant mood of lassitude. Families conversed quietly, young couples embraced, children slept in their mothers' laps. Henri dozed near Marta, not missing his nap after all. Even Marcel remained silent and supine, declining with a wave of his hand the last piece of Anne-Marie's cake.

Claire continued to be troubled by the drama she had just witnessed. She could not get the event out of her mind. Instead of relief she felt horror at what had only just been averted. How close they had all come to disaster! A few more seconds of unconsciousness and this carefree day would have turned into tragedy. The most banal moments of happiness were at the mercy of sudden treachery: a slippery riverbank, a patch of ice beneath a car. The seeming tranquillity of this ancient park camouflaged its steady slide towards its own demise. Life called for constant vigilance and alertness, Claire thought. Even if you were fortunate enough to stumble across a bit of happiness, part of you had to remain on guard, prepared for the moment when a stranger appeared carrying your child, lifeless, in his arms, or a policeman rang your bell to inform you that your mother had died in a car accident.

Soon it would be time to put away the remains of their picnic and think of the return journey, but for now no one seemed inclined to stir. The sound of human voices gave way to the buzzing of insects and the chatter of birds. The air was almost still. The wind, which had played havoc with napkins and empty paper cups earlier, now died down to a wayward breeze gently stirring the leaves in the trees above them. Claire looked around her and thought of a battlefield of pleasure with bodies lying where they had fallen in the action of the day. Only a few children remained upright, but they dragged their feet, as if some spell had transformed their wildly energetic play into lazy movement.

The happy scene of indolence puzzled her. She looked at Adrian stretched out beneath a tree, at her friends resting peacefully, and wondered, how did they do it? How did others manage to get on with life while she sat grieving, haunted by images of the child's limp, lifeless body, the mother's agony, the breathless anticipation of the crowd? And what was her grief about — losses to come? Her gaze returned to Adrian's face. Could she trust his change of heart, or would his reluctant acceptance of her desire for a child eventually turn to reproach?

Such painful considerations made it difficult for Claire to remain still. She rose quietly from her place and crept away. She longed for the comforting shelter of a secret retreat— a closed-off arbor of linden trees where she had spent so many hours of solitary pleasure. When she reached the overgrown arbor, she was pleased to find it unoccupied. Surrounded by dense, wild vegetation, it was almost invisible from the path. She sat down in a small clearing within the shelter of the linden trees, sinking into the embrace of the branches she had disturbed. The linden trees were in bloom and the perfume of their honey-scented flowers, so strong today, would always remind her of these gardens and the endless pots of *tilleul* she had shared with the countess, who allowed nothing to go to waste on her property. The perfume of the flowers was intoxicatingly voluptuous. It seemed to penetrate every pore of her skin, rendering her dizzy with its sweetness.

Her thoughts turned to a favorite passage in one of Rousseau's letters. The words, retrieved from memory, went straight to her heart. "The places we have loved remain with us accompanying us wherever we go. In my lifetime I spent many years in exile running from the wrath of one despot or another. Alone and far from all I loved, I would ease my weary soul recalling scenes of nature that formerly brought great joy to me: the splendor of mountains I had climbed in my youth, a field of wildflowers where I had rested on a fiercely hot afternoon, the still mountain lakes where I learned to swim as a boy, a grove of trees that had sheltered me from the rain. All these I carried with me wherever I fled and they have never failed to comfort me. With the passing of time, we have only the faintest memory of those we have loved and who loved us. That is the way of the human heart. But nature is constant and remains a solace for all time."

The familiar words calmed her when she was startled to hear approaching footsteps. It was rare to come across anyone in this isolated spot and instinctively she moved deeper into the vegetation. At that moment the wind stirred again and the groaning of the tree branches camouflaged all other sounds. She wondered if the intruder had passed. Suddenly she heard Adrian calling her name. His presence astonished her. How on earth had he found her? Was it possible he remembered her description of this favorite spot and looked for her here? The happiness she suddenly felt was her answer. He had listened to her words and they had led him to her. It was wonderfully reassuring to think this vast park could not conceal her from him. Claire walked towards the path and the sound of Adrian's voice.

"I'm happy you found me," she told him, rewarding him with a loving embrace.

"Me too. I have something to tell you." She noticed an air of excitement about him that usually signaled a breakthrough in his work. No doubt he had solved some problem since she had left him sitting under a tree. But Adrian wasn't speaking of work: "You know that awful moment when we were all waiting to see if the child would breathe again? It was so intense, I could feel my heart pounding painfully. It reminded me of your description of a panic attack. I wondered if I was having a sympathy attack. I couldn't understand my response. Then it dawned on me. I was reacting as a parent would, not as a concerned spectator who would soon forget the incident. That child could be ours."

She looked up and saw the emotion in his face, felt it in the way his hands pressed into her shoulders. "Oh Claire, life is terrifying and unpredictable. And having children makes the odds worse. And yet, the moment I understood my response, I felt a sense of intense elation, the kind you feel on the brink of a grand adventure. That's what I came to tell you."

Claire leaned against Adrian, marveling once again at the power exerted by the tiny being growing inside her, still only centimeters in size. The quiet of the moment was broken by the sound of a jet ascending into the sky. She watched it disappear from sight, wishing she was on it, flying home, flying towards her future, as invisible and inevitable as the plane's swift journey somewhere in the immense vastness of space.